There is
always
something
more

Also by Che Chidi Chukwumerije

Poetry:
Palm Lines
The Beautiful Ones have been born
Writing is the Happiness of Sorrow
Light of Awakening
River
Cumbrian Lines: poems born of the lake district
Mmiri a zoro nwayo nwayo (Poems in igbo)
Innengart (Poems in german)
Das dauerhafte Gedicht (Poems in german)

Prose:
Twice is not enough
The Lake of Love

For children:
Somayinozo's Stories

Che Chidi Chukwumerije
There is always something more
Second Edition 2015.
First edition 2012 under the pseudonym Aka Teraka.
Boxwood Publishing House e.K.
Copyright © Che Chidi Chukwumerije 2012
All rights reserved
ISBN 978-3-943000-72-6

Che Chidi Chukwumerije

...

There Is Always Something More

...

Boxwood Publishing House, Frankfurt

Table of Contents

1: Struggling with the dawn

2: Songs of the wanderer

3: When I look within

i.

Struggling with
the dawn

...

Remember The Sun, Look Up

...

ONCE UPON a time, there was a bird.

It flew and flew for a long time, over great distances, over lakes, mountains and forests, over deserts, countries and valleys, over vast oceans and across mighty fields of thought.

One day, as it was flying over such a field of thought, it looked down and saw a little girl playing in the red-brown soil of Owerri, a small town in south-eastern Nigeria. Dressed in a short, tie-dyed west African boubou and skipping merrily on bare feet behind her father's house, the little girl threw thoughts up into the air, bright blue and yellow thoughts, the way other children throw up ribbons and balls. And when the thoughts went into the air, they would take wing and fly high into the sky, so high up that not even the bird could see the height into which they soared.

One by one they would then, after a long while, re-appear in the visible firmament as they began their downward flight to the girl. Upon their descent the thoughts were bigger, brighter, more beautiful, and they all bore a crown on their heads. This the bird could see.

By the time the thoughts returned to the girl, her father's house had washed away and she had grown into a woman, a young and beautiful woman with a silent sorrow on her face, a deep question in her eyes, a lovely, innocent yet knowing smile upon her lips. For in the period in which her thoughts had flown to heaven, many men and women had loved and left her. Some had loved her too little and some had loved her too much. But none had loved her enough. Now she stood there with the universal question in her heart; the search for her destiny.

A song. Beautiful was the song that came out of the bird, descended along with the woman's return-ing thoughts. One by one, her thoughts alighted on her breast, folded their wings around her like in an embrace and dissolved into her. As each thought dis-appeaed back into her, her eyes became brighter, the sadness upon her ebony features faded away, little by little, the question gradually disappeared, and she gradually grew up... until the last thought had reunited itself with her, and she stood there, tall, pretty, mature, clear.

Then did she hear the song... the song of the bird... it pierced her heart like a bird's beak penetrating into the heart of a wild honey flower and told her wild and gentle stories of things forgotten and remembered. Like the sunflower her heart exploded open and she looked up...

And she saw the sun!

And while she revelled in the sight of the sun, for since attaining adulthood she had not noticed the sun anymore, the bird flapped it's wings again and flew on, flew away. By the time the woman, filled with the sun, looked around in the sky for the source of the lovely song that made her look up in the first place and awakened her to the sun..., the bird was long gone.

Once upon a time, there was a bird... on and on it flew, over fields of thought and gentle growth. Simple is her song:

Remember the sun, look up -

The Old Book

...

I SOUGHT MY daughter whom I had not seen for hours now. It was already at the start of that unfailing daily event called Sunset. I sat down outside the little bungalow; well, I call it a bungalow, I'm sure there are some who'll call it a hut. I was happy, but a certain restlessness stirred in my soul. Maybe she was playing in the woods downhill; I could imagine her admiring and memorizing the shapes and colours of all the wild flowers and little insects in the bushes, her enduring passion. She would soon be back.

The sun, setting, was beautiful. I saw him playing with the clouds lazily travelling by. The wind tickled the whispering grasses, and I was alone.

I liked this new bungalow of mine, perched on this

hilltop, giving me a true view of the entire country-side, the village, and those ancient forbidden caves in the distance of which all kinds of impossible tales are still told even until today; yes, this hilltop and this bungalow up here had a strong hold on me, unlike the old hut further down in the valley where I had been born, where I had grown up.

I missed my wife and longed for her return. She had travelled a hundred kilometers away to care for her sick mother for a few days, leaving our daughter and me alone until she would return.

My mind slipped to my childhood back in the old hut. To my brothers and sisters, my parents and old friends. Everybody was gone now. The old ones had died. The young ones had grown up and moved away. Only I had remained here on these hilly south-eastern plains. Now I lived with my wife and daughter in a new bungalow, well to be honest, a big hut really, on a hill, not far from the old one, the last keeper of our culture. For some reason, my heart just could not de-tach from these environs. Born freely to farm my vil-lage lands, I did just that everyday, walking down into the village, then beyond it, to our ancestral farmlands. This week had been a quiet week, though, as I stayed at home with my daughter and waited for my wife to return from her mother .

It started to grow dark. My thoughts came back to the present. I began to worry. Where was my daughter?

Then she was there...

I saw dimly her fragile lithe form slowly mounting the gentle slope, a small basket clutched to her side. Normally she ran, hopped and skipped. I hoped she was not feeling ill.

I let her come to me. I heard her footsteps. Then I saw her face – drawn... her eyes wide, starring... - something was wrong.

"Neanya!" I gasped, springing up.

She walked on straight towards me, her widened eyes never leaving mine, as though searching for answers, a hold, *something*. What? And then suddenly, a few paces away from me, she abruptly stopped. I walked quickly up to her, bent down, held her; just eight years old; she stood stiffly; her eyes were white.

"Neanya," I whispered, "What's wrong? Did something happen? What happened? Tell me!"

She took a deep breath, swallowed. Still these questioning eyes gripping mine. An uneasy apprehension began to grow within me. With a quick glance I briefly scanned the declining grassland behind her; saw nothing, nobody.

"Neanya..." I began again. Her lips parted.

She spoke. A whisper:

"I saw... a... strange man – "

"Who? *Where?*"

"Down the hill, near the old hut, behind the forest... on that other path that leads to the farmlands..."

"What were you looking for there? I thought you were on the edge of the forest."

"After playing with the flowers in the forest, I went to the other side, to the giant *ụdara* tree, I was hoping to pick some ripe and fallen *ụdara* berries... for you."

I looked into her basket, expecting it to be empty. It was full of *ụdara*. I stretched out my hands, one reaching for the basket, the other her shoulder. She veered away, but remained standing where she was, her basket of wild berries still pressed against her body.

Silence.

"And *what happened?*"

"He was very sad, father. He was crying."

"A strange man? Crying? Where?"

"By the woods, downhill, near the old hut... he was not an old man... he was crying..."

Her answers came in phrases. Her eyes still gripped mine. *Something* had happened. *But what?*

"So I held his hand – "

"You *what?* Neanya! *Who* was he? What did he do to you?"

But she simply continued as though I had not interrupted her.

" – and asked him why he was crying. He looked at me, father, and he was sad. And then... he smiled a little. He said... he said..."

"What did he say?"

"He said that I looked familiar – "

"And have you seen him before?"

For the first time the starry look in Neanya's eyes dispersed somewhat. I could see she was thinking. Eight years old; *what* was she thinking about?

"I don't know, father... but he looked very familiar too – "

All at once I felt very uncomfortable, psychically and physically, as if I was subject to a strange, invisible pressure. My throat went dry. I swallowed, took a deep breath and said slowly to my daughter:

"Now Neanya, just tell me *everything! What happened?* What did this stranger *tell* you?"

Standing as though rooted to the spot, my daughter looked at me for a few seconds with that thoughtful, questioning glow in her eyes again, and then, after what seemed like a moment of consideration, nodded and slowly began to speak.

"He said he was trapped there, that he could not move on... that's what he said... because, he said, he said that he had been torn by guilt, he had..." She paused a while, breathe deeply once, then continued. "He had... killed himself when he was *on earth,* that's what he said, that he rejected the gift of earthlife God gave him..." She paused, took another deep breath, quietly exhaled. She seemed to be thinking, yet for a second I almost had the impression... that she was *listening.*

16

Then, with a sigh, and a slight nod, she continued:

"And... and he said that amongst other things he did not stay to take care of his only child... and that now he is torn by even greater guilt... that's exactly what he said, father... - he said he wants me to go to his child today, right away, Father, to tell his child that... that...," she choked, stopped.

"What?" I whispered. Was this a dream? Had the imaginative powers of her mind gone too far?

"He told me to go to his child – "

I shook my head and held Neanya's shoulders.

"Ssssh. Sssshh. Sssssshhh. You've had a bad day-dream, that's – "

"He even told me his child's name, father, and where I could go to find him this evening," Neanya whispered, interrupting me gently and raising her eyes to the sky. Her eyes were suddenly old. The sky was a deep dark blue and, all around us, the night crickets were chirping.

"What is his child's name?"

"Norondu – "

My heart stopped beating.

"Is that not your name, Father?" whispered Neanya, her eyes coming back down from distant skies and reclaiming mine. "Is that not what Mummy calls you?"

My heart had still not started beating.

... My biological father had died when I was a baby. I had grown up with my mother and stepfather and

their children, my half-brothers and -sisters. I had never known what my original father died of. I only knew he had been some kind of restless adventurer travelling through the lands. I always assumed he died by some kind of accident. People did not like speaking much about him...

"What did the man want you to tell Norondu?" I whispered to Neanya.

"That the old Book of Knowledge which his grandfather had given to *his* father, and his father had given to him, ... is buried exactly beneath the spot on which I am now standing... - "

Sunrise

...

THE BEGINNING IS the end.

Dawn is just about to break, I awaken from a deep sleep. The sleep was dark, I dreamt of demons and devils running after me. My life is at its lowest ebb. I am unhappy.

Tired I rise to my feet, slowly limp out of my hut, into the little dirt track dragging its way across the outer hamlets far away from the nearest, secluded, village. Dim twilight prevails. My head hangs and the story of my life briefly replays itself in my memory.

I remember the child, carefree, sanguine. The happy family that was its home, the humble abode that housed their love. The carefreeness.

I remember standing up like an impatient tree into

manhood, searching for the sun, but my crown got lost in the dizzying clouds, pregnant with temptation. Then came the fall.

It was not the bacteria that killed my wife, it was the aching heart that closed its eyes to me, full of regret and disappointment. It was not the whispers of untrue friends that led my children astray, but the missing guidance of a self-absorbed father. It was not my friends who abandoned me, but I who abandoned what I could have been. Even my foes deserted me, they have nothing left to shame. Twenty years later, I emerge, destitute, beggar, soulless, lifeless, into the cool dark morning before the sun...

Dawn is for new beginnings. The hour before dawn shall be my coronation. Death. And should dawn come before, then let me start anew on the other side. These are my thoughts this morning, dark fruits of that dream. For once in your life be a man, and put an end to it.

Wearily I return into the hut. For some reason I wait until I smell it. Then I re-emerge into the slow brightening twilight of fore-dawn, a dagger in my hand. Why exactly have I come out into the open to do it? I do not know. Maybe simply because I want to die facing the sky, the big all-seeing eye.

Poised and ready, one last time scenes from my life rush like a highspeed freight-train across the charred landscape of my memory, then I raise my blade, firm, gripping with both hands... point it towards my innards... I close my eyes.

No last prayer awakens in my soul. No final thought. No closure. All I want is the deep dark plunge, the sharp pain, the flowing warmth of exit, the blurred eternity of death.

That moment when you are about to say goodbye to a familiar place, when you stand on the hilltop like Lot's wife, knowing you should hurry on, don't look back, yet unable to resist the last goodbye. It is the moment of betrayal that brings about the reversal of fortune. How long did I perch on the brink of that moment, looking at the end of my life?

Everything drew itself into one spot, like a raincloud, and suddenly it was time. I bend my knees, steel myself for the hard, fast plunge into the lightless waterfall. Did I breathe in or out? ...

Dimly, as though from far away, I hear footsteps.

Footsteps?

Footsteps? I have never heard footsteps down in these deserted outlands, at such an early hour, before. Am I sure? Have I heard right? I wish to set off on my journey into solitude... in solitude.

I listen. For a long time I hear nothing. My resolve is not brittle, it turns around again and refocuses on its way. But, softly, I hear them again – slightly louder.

Footsteps. Yes. Frozen like a statue, I manage to blink a few moments later when he appears... an old man with a walking rod, his head completely bald. I recognise him. It is the hermit.

My knees are still bent, the cold steel still points to me, the sacrifice, when he reaches me. He stops. He looks at me in the grey twilight. I see a look of surprise grow on his face.

"Son?..." he asks, starled. "What are you doing?"

I look into his eyes. Within me something akin to emotion refuses to stir. Serenely I say:

"I am about to kill myself, oh hermit..."

"To *kill* yourself?" I hear the surprise also in his voice. "But why"

Serenely still, I reply:

"My life is empty, meaningless. I have lost it all, wife, family, everything. Friends, money, life's work. With them went my *will* to work too. Now I too must depart."

It is an odd feeling to speak into eyes that steadily grow softer the harder your words become. It is quite distracting, because you begin to wonder why.

"My son, are you satisfied with this decision?"

"Indeed, oh hermit, I am."

He smiled, as though he were the keeper of a secret.

"But child – "

"You have lived twice the length of my life, it is true,

yet call me not child, for I do know what I am doing."

"It is not knowing what you are doing that matters, my son, but knowing *why* you are doing what you are doing."

Thought is the enemy of blind resolve. Why is he talking to me? Obligating me to a logical answer. A trap. I cannot kill myself until I free myself from it. For conviction, standing on irrefutable clarity, is my justifier. This proud I am, and he knows it. I see it in his amused eyes watching mine, challenging me to convince him too. I mustn't, I know. But it seems to me the last duty I owe a failed life. I want to die proudly. Nobody had ever asked me this question. I want to find the answer to it before I go, not for him but for me, that I may go in peace. Everybody might plain know what he is doing – but the deeper reason? Did I not know it?

I am a bit irritated by the fact that no clear-cut answer jumps out of my observant soul immediately, and that I have to think it out. It makes me a bit uneasy, such a simple statement.

My arms lower under the weight of thought, I raise them up again, reposition the blade. I wish I had not done that, for he notices everything, down to my thoughts and the movement in my heart. I can see it in his curious eyes.

"But I know very well why I am doing what I am doing, oh hermit."

"Why, child?"

"I have already said it all to you, but I will flesh it out now, father. You see, I had a beautiful childhood, a quiet youth, the journey of manhood began well. I married a beautiful woman. I had no reason to stray from the path. But I did. In the beginning I had life, now I have lifelessness. I have heard that the beginning is the end, but not in my life. My life ends in nothing. My beloved wife is dead, she died from the inner loneliness and pain into which I thrust her. My sons and daughters are monsters and thieves. My people have ostracized me, my friends deserted me, my wealth squandered, my fame evaporated.

"Even enemies... Hermit, do you know what it means when enemies no longer concern themselves with one? That is the ultimate mark of meaninglessness."

"Don't you think you can start all over again?" asks the hermit tenderly. "Start afresh? Pick up the threads? Build anew?" His tone, though tender, is conversational, as if we were talking about the weather.

I shake my head, I'm not sure if wearily or angrily.

"No, hermit, there are no threads to pick up. There is no foundation upon which to build anew. I must go. These reasons suffice."

"Life is a gift, my friend," says the hermit. "Measure it not according to what happens on the outside, but by the forces within your soul. And there is so much life in your soul, my son. This I see."

His words are getting too close to home. I am trying to block them out, but it is not easy. They are penetrant, threatening to inject into me a dose of reflection. Seeds of new life, warmth, vitality. But I don't want the pain that comes with the warmth. I don't want the exertion that the vitality demands. I don't want the new thoughts of reflection that a fresh lease of life would bring. I am afraid.

Afraid. Surprised I gaze at this recognition, almost amused, wondering how and why I missed that point all along. Quickly following upon the trite amusement is seriousness, as I feel my consciousness slip into the pool of fear in which my subconscious has been drowning all along. I am afraid. I had all these things before and I wandered away, into the darkness. No. Let me alone. I don't want life that will remind me of my sins, and demand that I atone, and put me back on the crossroad where I fell before, demanding that I choose *again*.

Oh, no. I fear.

Leave me alone in my pitifulness and self-pity. Leave me in my dejection and self-pity. I don't want responsibility. My inner life is weak. I don't want to take another shot at life. I might lose again. I want to die.

Like bolts of lightning, flashes of clarity, these thoughts, these intuitive perceptions surge through me, shaking me. Goodbye and welcome. He is smiling, the hermit! I have to face him one last time.

"Let me be, Hermit," I breathe out wearily. "I am a nobody, a nothing, life has passed me by, I am finished. Depression and despair are all I have now. The deep clear confusion of seeing no way forward. "

"If you see no way forward, then stand still... but don't plunge into the abyss."

I shake my head. "I am tired... of life."

Now he shakes his head. "I would put it differently. I would say that you have merely *decided* that you are tired of life. Is that not so?"

For a moment our eyes remained locked on each other. Then, without warning, he turns back to the road and begins to walk away, continuing on his journey. The sun is pushing up from the valley, the hermit reaches the hill's zenith and then quickly begins to descend. I watch him disappear, the sun appear.

Now I look down at the knife which I still hold in my hand. Curious, but I'm suddenly wandering why exactly I picked it up in the first place.

The Presence

. . .

NEWLY THE sun shone anew. Happy the multitude was to see again their surroundings. But where were they? A no-land. Only space and space and space. But no footprints and not a voice on the wind.

We seek the voices, we hear the silence. The multitude is faced with the choice – to turn inwards or to turn outwards. The multitude turned inwards and became a nation. Generations later, the nation turned outwards and faced the world.

Thus was the first Pride born. For the nation was too much for the world.

Let us leave the world and the nation, the multitude,

the space and the silence, and look at the street. A busy street. Hawkers, traders, pedestrians, beggars, jam the sidewalks. Busses, cars, motorcycles, cram the roads.

Above them, an unsmiling face, almost but not as large as the sky, looks down guardingly upon them. The face is not the face of a loving protector, that much can be deduced from its features. It is the face of a prison warden. Emotionless and evil. Because the prison is his.

A face turns upwards. One of the people on the street has a strange sensation hard to describe. She looks up, sees the face, screams and collapses. People walk by her. Others stop. She is dead. They cross themselves, mutter prayers and walk away.

Let us go back to the nation. The nation has arisen. It is all-powerful. It runs like a well-oiled machine, a high-tec computer. It shut itself out of the world for generations. It let nothing in, not even nature. Now it is ready to face the world. It towers over the rest of the world and opposes all who seek to break away from this new sway.

Others raise their gazes too, see the face of the guardian of evil. They collapse and die too, just like the woman. But the souls of the dead have risen too, they mingle amongst the living and strengthen invisibly their resolve. And sometimes now when I look up at the giant face of the prison-guard in the dark dark clouds above us, I see a slightly worried look in his eyes. Things are going wrong. He feels it. But he cannot put his finger on it.

Why are people looking up?

The Way

...

I WAS wondering in the dark, searching for my hands, for my feet, my voice, my mind. I sought all these things, but knew not that I was searching in the dark. In a strange valley that wipes away memory. Truly I was wandering too in the dark.

There are friends that stand around us in the dark, more in number than we know, nearer than we sense, they see us but we do not see them. For, self-centred us, we see only ourselves.

There was a self-centred man, and he never saw anything but himself. His own wants, his own needs, his own hopes, his own fears, his own hunger and thirst, his own pain, joy, views, his own creed.

There he was, wandering in the dark, lonely and

alone, thinking he is all alone in the world. Not once does the thought of another cross his mind, for he has long lost the ability to see any other person but himself. A hundred questions trouble his mind, to which he finds no answers. It is dark. Some helpers stand around him, trying to draw his attention for once away from his own ego, for these helpers have the answers he craves. But he sees them not; he has long lost the ability to see any other but himself.

What are these rocks that strike and bleed his feet? He knows not, he sees them not. The light with which to see them is not visible to him. He sees only himself, nothing else. His inner eyes are closed, where is the insight with which to see the inner light? A misty lake has become his insight; therein, trapped, his egotistical love for himself.

So did we wander side by side for decades, centuries, blind to one another, unconscious of each another, for each of us was self-centered. Slowly I started to long for an end to this grey solitude, this heavy empty aloneness. Then did a thought, dimly, strike me, in the depths of my lonely suffering. The thought that this lonely life I led was so sad, so depressing that I would never wish it for anybody else....

- stop. What was that?

Anybody else? ... What strange thought is this that strikes me? Is there anything like *somebody else?* Am I not alone in the world? Could there be any other person here? Struggling in this dark blindness too? A strange new thought that nagged at, and grew in, my heart. If there were anybody else, then would that I could find him, maybe even help him, halve his frustration. - Like a miracle, this thought became a light within me, slowly did my inner eye open.

And... I saw myself in a Valley... walking beside a man who seemed faintly familiar, with the soft sun shinning far away, dimly but visibly. But though I called and called to him, this strangely familiar man, yet he heard me not, felt not my touch. And lo and behold, not he alone, but hundreds, thousands, millions like us were wandering blind in the Valley of Self-centeredness. Unreachable. Alone. I had been simply one of many all this time and I had not known. So deep was my shock that it loosened my heart and set my tears free. Only half the tears were for me. The rest were for my fellow wanderers, as blinded by self-centeredness as I had until recently been. And yet all they need in order to awaken is just once to think of another... spare a thought for another. Focus again on the thought that there are also other people in this world, think of their needs, feel the desire to understand and to help someone else.

After the tears had started to flow from my eyes, I heard a voice. There was a woman walking behind me.

"Did you say something to me?", I asked, surprised,

as I turned to her. She had a voice like a bird singing. She too I seemed to almost remember.

"Osahon, my friend", she said, "I have been calling your name now for many many decades, patiently trying to awaken you to the way that leads out of this Valley wherein you have been groping..."

"You?... Calling me for *decades?* Has it been that long? Yet I heard nothing..."

"It is because you have stepped off the way."

"And where lies the way?" I asked, still dazed, still grappling this new awakening.

And she pointed to my neighbour, he who had been by my side all this time, unnoticed by me, unconscious of me.

"Walk with him a couple of miles. Find out what he needs, and try to give it to him. Therein lies the way."

"But who is he?" I asked.

"That is Erobo. You were his friend, to whom he once looked up, once upon a time..., like I too once was your star, before we both went blind. Before the bird came to wake me up again. Long long ago. Do you remember?" -

Like a mist slowly parting did I gently recall distant friendships, selfless love, ancient, bright sunlight once upon a time. And as I did, so did the Valley become ever brighter, for this faint Sun had always been there. Only I had gone blind.

"This is what happens," my ancient lover continued, "when self-centeredness takes over within the soul. So do memory, connection and awareness fade... This is what happens when self-centeredness takes over within our souls."

I gazed at Efe, my one true love. How could I have forgotten her all this time? ... Then I turned and beheld once more my very best friend, Erobo, he who had once been to me even as a brother. Softly I called his name, then louder, until I was shouting it. And yet he heard not.

"He hears you not," Efe sorrowfully said. "He hears only his own thoughts, and knows not that any other thing exists. And all this he once learned from you," she said softly to me, "For he has always followed you. Yet wipe your eyes, stand by his side and keep on calling his name... Weary not, but love him even as you love yourself."

At first I felt a sense of guilt. I reflected upon this mystery: You can lead a man in, but not out. The thought of an unending, unrewarding sojourn beside an unresponsive soul suddenly brought a hesitation upon me. I looked at the multitude of sleepwalkers around me in the valley, and saw behind so many of them a Helper, bound to each as by an invisible thread, trying to reach them. Tenacious thoughts. They arose again in me. What of my own goals? What of my own wants? A frown, a dark cloud came over my brow, I slowly sunk into brooding

"Osahon... my friend – "

Startled I looked up. My gaze, as from far away, set-tled again upon Efe. Her hand was upon my shoulder. A smile was her face. A sad smile, it pierced my core. And then did drop the last chain. I turned again to Erobo, my best friend, placed a hand on his shoulder and began to talk to him, calling his name, telling him of the sun and of friendship and of helpfulness and of the way out of the Valley. Out of my words I made a song, which I am still singing...

"And should he one day awaken and his blind eyes open before Time bids you stop," my Lover continued, her last words to me, before she left to go there where she must await me, " ... and should he then weary too of selfishness, and desire a way out of this half-lit Val-ley, then show him also this Way which I have just shown to you, teach it to him gently, and remind him of it should he quickly forget too... - for there is no other way that leads out of this Valley, but the way of selfless love."

Then I saw her walking away, following a distant bird. When I weary I think of her and of her selfless love; and thus, I too am still talking to my friend.

Ihụnanya

...

I STAND upon a cloud, detached and unnoticed, and look down at the gentle green hillocks of Isuochi, those last scattered foothills of the Udi hillrange in south-eastern Nigeria. On one of the most secluded and hidden hinter knolls is a hut. No, a cave. Masterfully blended into the mounded cocoon of the hummock with that subtle touch of which only nature is capable, it bears on its rough back an assembly of wild-haired *ụdara* trees huddled as though in conference about the destiny of the old man in the cave beneath their roots, one who has for decades made this removed grotto his home. Around the cave, all is still. Nothing stirs; nobody in sight. But I know he is there, in the cave, silent, communing with himself, the old man in the hills. I know it well, feel it deep, for once upon a time, I was he.

But that was long ago, before love seized his heart and ground it to bits, scattering the gold-dust of his longings into the gathering arms of the wind who collected them greedily only to scatter then again with childish abandon, hoping he would never again find them. He blew them to the ends of the earth... where they simply re-gathered, *recollected*, his love and pain, his yearning heart, glued together by remorse; like phoenix, arising anew. Slowly, with time, they found their way back to him, their origin, as though pulled by a memory magnet. Like a guardian they float above his cave in the harmattan sunset of his life now, steering him... even though he does not know that I do so. Yes, once upon a time we were one.

But now he is much wiser. The substance of his life and the love that purified him, purified his inmost soul in excrutiating pain, had been so powerful that when it was over he had been freed of passion and pain, desire and death, reduced in the crucible of experiencing into a wise man. While I, his passion and pain, the living form of his invisible regret, watch now over him from above his head, yearning for release and dissolution even as much as I yearn for him, the lonely old man. No, not lonely, only alone. The wise man in the hills. A long story of love and pain brought him to this place and this state of being, a long story that cleansed his heart and then poured runes of recognition from the vials of Solomon into the emptied coffers.

As I stand upon the cloud today I feel more heavily than ever the pain of all the experiences we went through, the ache of glaring clarity. Oh, could this agony but ease off a little... a moment of teaching mediated to another wanderer at the crossroads where we too once stood. What is the essence of love? When it has conquered you, you understand.

Dusk approaches, the sun sets, the beautiful sun. I watch him silently depart into the graveyard of night. Always, he keeps his thoughts to himself. The sun has just disappeared... night has fallen. Riding atop my cloud, I descend lower, closer to the cool night earth. The warmth of the buried sun's radiance still permeates my being like the memory of a delicious meal. I sense that tonight there'll be a difference. I sense movement within the cave. The old man stirs, awakens, seeking fulfilment.

And then he appears. Tall, firm. Strong, erect. He holds his head up like the noon sun, but cocked slightly to one side. He walks slowly, with easy deliberation, like a king, away from the trees, into the open. His eyes look into the distance, filled with a searching look that arose out of his vast heart. When a man has sinned and in the process set a wrong precedence, maybe through his children or grandchildren an opportunity will one day present itself through which he may atone. Like tonight. I see it coming and I wait. Years have passed since he made the grave mistake that gave birth to me, his love and pain juxtaposed. Will I finally dissolve again tonight? I wait.

And then I see from far away a figure, a shadow of light, approaching, ascending the gradient.

Who?

It is Kulie, walking slowly, but resolutely. It takes him almost an hour. But finally, he arrives the tor. He looks up at me, but he sees only the cloud. Me he sees not. I am higher than eyes can see.

I study Kulie as he stoically traces the tracks of the lonesome wise man in the foothills. I observe Kulie. A handsome, young man. Spitting image of his great-grand-father, the mad man in the foothills.

A moment of silence... then Kulie comes upon the wise man, my wise man, standing iroko-erect, backing the world.

Kulie stands still. He speaks not. All his life he has heard of the madman in the foothills, his great-grand-father, unseen by human eyes now for almost two decades, fuelling speculation that he had finally died. But Kulie's inner voice had told him that he lived yet. And now he saw him here standing before him. Why have I come?, Kulie thinks to himself. He cannot answer himself. Yet he knows that he acted right.

Slowly the wise man turns. His eyes, burning like

the red hot coal in the bowels of these ancient hill-range, pierce Kulie's soul. Kulie yields not, stares back. Before him he sees a tall, thin, very dark complexioned and very old man. His shirtless torso hangs thinly on his proud skeleton above half-trousers that reach down to just below his knees. His feet are bare. His cheek bones stick out like hard balls upon an impassive face. Only the eyes burn.

"Kulie..." begins the wise man, "*Gwam!* Tell me. Why have you risked your life and reputation by coming here?" Kulie is at first taken aback by the old man's directness which leaves no room for a proper traditional greeting. And how come the man knows his name?? All this shoots through his mind as he takes in this voice which seems to spread out, as though trying to permeate the world. "You want people to castigate you for communing with an outcasted, mad, man?" His igbo is refined, royal.

Kulie bows his head for a second. Still he shifts not. Promptly he raises his eyes again.

"*Nna anyị*... our father," says Kulie in a strong voice, "I am confused."

"And what confuses you?" asks the wise man softly.

"Love, sir..." replies Kulie, "Only love. *Ịhụnanya*."

Calm, like the closing of an umbrella when the rain is done, descends anew upon the wise man. Yes, now he is sure. Kulie is the promised one.

"Speak your heart, son," says the wise man, "Simply your heart."

Kulie decides to say it simply, the best way to say some things.

"It is the Cause, father, the one that was first started by you. It has awakened in my heart too. It has landed on the table of my destiny and I don't know what to do. A great love for the people has seized my heart. It has become my cause, like it once was yours. I am ready to work just for the people, to live and die for them. I have proven this to them many times. They know my love, and they have loved me back.

"But... hurtful has been their love, father. They have often turned away at decisive crossroads; often reciprocated my sacrifices, now with gratitude, now with scorn; often chosen empty promisers of illusion over me, until their hopes were dashed, and then come running back to me... until the next liar showed up again. This has been the cycle for years now, such that now... now... I do not know any longer whether or not this Cause and I really belong together. Maybe I am not the right one for it, nor it the right one for me. And yet I cannot abandon it. I just cannot stop trying to get the people to wholeheartedly follow the path of development and growth. They say yes to me with their lips, sometimes with their eyes too... yet the harder I pull, the more lukewarm they seem to become. From afar they cheer me on. But none wants to walk the path with me. I doubt that they really appreciate the effort, yet my love is so great, I keep on accommodating their lukewarmness.

"And I ask myself: This thing that sits so uneasy in my hand, is it really mine, or am I just forcing the whole issue, pushed by selfish ambition? It obsesses me, but I can't seem to make any headway. Do you understand? I want it, but does it want me?"

A moon appears from behind a cloud and brightly illuminates the wise man's face... briefly. The sharp, burning, deepset eyes... the flared, angry nose... the rugged lines of fate running down his forehead, knifing their way into the bridge of his nose... the rocky cheek bones... his glowing countenance was an ebonine wood-carving hung on eternity's canvas.

And his voice says something very simple. Something he once read but did not understand when he needed it the most, something he has always wanted to plant, like a seed, into the heart of someone who stands too at the crossroad but, unlike he, will understand:

"Kulie... when you love something, set it free," his voice rises, trembles, his eyes look up, "If it comes back to you, son, then it is yours. But if it does not, then it never was."

For long, long moments, as silence whistles through his heart, Kulie stands looking at a man who has turned round again, backing the earth afresh. In Kulie's heart he understands. But it's so painful, too difficult... *letting go*. He opens his mouth to complain, to quest further –

But the voice of the wise man suddenly rips through the hilltop anew.

"*Ngwa*, Kulie! Go... and be a man! Free yourself."

And as though the words were a presence by themselves, a force propels Kulie away. He hurries down the incline, his heart burning for his cause.

When you love something, set it free!

Higher climbs the moon, full. Midnight approaches. Maybe Kulie will do the right things. The words were sparse, but the wise man knows that they are exactly what Kulie needs, that he will understand the message at the heart of them. The wise man is free of half of his burden.

Now the other approaches. He bounces up and down the foothills, slowly mounting up the gradient. I look into his face – I see selfishness and inconsideration. I feel a pang of pain stab through me. I seek for the gentleness and love of Kulie in his soul, find them not. Finally, he arrives the hummock.

Again, like Kulie, his eyes first seek the cloud upon which I stand, detached and unnoticed. His name is Jideofor. I know him well, the absolute reflection of that which I used to be. If Kulie is the wise man, then Jideofor is me.

He charges straight for the wise man who faces the

moon. I notice an air of reluctance hanging around him.

"Yes?" Tersely. "*Ọ gịnị?*" Without turning around.

"I knew that I had to come here. So I did."

Now the wise man turns, looks. Yes, it is he.

"And what is your problem?"

Jideofor grimaces. "It is the people, your people! I love them but I am tired of it all. Why do they complain all the time? Why do they demand all the time. I give and give all I can, yet they never stop demanding, like a bunch of greedy, ungrateful children. They are always irritable. I have outwitted all their enemies, all our enemies, and brought development to the community, and yet they keep demanding, demanding. In other places, people would worship me if I gave them just half of what I have given this people, our people, your people! Fighting your lost cause. But they remain unsatisfied. Truly, I have come to the end of this road!"

The wise man's voice is cold as ice:

"Jideofor! *Gee ntị.* Listen very carefully, I will say this only once. When you love something, cherish it. Keep it close to your heart. Cherish it. Do not even slightly ease up your hold on it... or it will fly away and never come back back!

"Do you understand?"

Like a thunderclap his voice slams into Jideofor's soul, sending him careening down the hill like a dislodged boulder, seeking his fate.

When you love something, hold it tight!

The wise man sighs. His life is over. He has atoned.
The two faces of love have been voiced and released
into two hearts and into the ether, never to die again.
He walks back to his cave. The fire in his eyes, it has
died. His body lets out its last breath. His spirit flies
away. Home. His remains will have his hill for a grave,
his cave for a gravestone. The wild arms of his beloved *ụdara* trees wave him goodbye in the harmattan wind.

In the sky above the ghostly silhouette of trees on
the knoll there glows a lovely fullbloomed moon; riding beneath it on his cloud, slowly dispersing at last, is
my pacified self; the shadow of the wise man's heart;
his regret; his remorse; his longing to atone; his burning desire to make good, thawing at last. Reflecting
these two so different explanations to love, seemingly
contradictory – to let go, or to hold on.

Two views, two songs, two sides.

And the people, trapped in the cause, understand
not as Kulie and Jideofor relate and act out the dif-
fering messages they each claimed to have received
from their great-grandfather in the same night. It
seems like a contradiction to the people, another evi-
dence of that old outcast's state of mind. The different
voices of this one simple truth told by the wise man

elicit divergent responses from various souls.

Some call it insanity. A few dub it amnesia. Others call it agony, pain.

But I, I call it the Understanding.

Insomnia

...

THERE IS A frenzy in the air. The world is dark and bloody like an ominous sunset. The land is full of cogitation. Everybody is fired up, wired up, wound up like an electric train, toy trains on their permanently defined tracks. There is a sad desperation in their every chug and hoot, in their every wailing whistle, a longing for a freedom that will never be, must never be, because this freedom, freedom from these tracks, this prison, would mean the end of destiny, the termination of purpose and of life.

This is the continuum in which I live. A dark and dirty cocoon. But who dares to break out? Who dares risking the encountering of the recognition that, truly, all one might be is a toy e-train on toy tracks mounted on a table in the children's playroom? Who shall risk this dare, in the hope of finding another reality, the celebration of birth of butterfly?

A longing, hard to define, was long the taproot. The root of roots and hope of hopes. The dream unre-membered in the clamour of urban dawn. Generation gap after generation gap. Yawning emptiness. Your blood is much too soggy. It weighs you down and is choking you to death, dear continuum. You are more than city, more than state, more than country, more than region, subregion, continent or subcontinent, even you are more than world. You are continuum. And I hate you. Hate you for holding me, for binding me, for being an extension of me and a limitation of me. I hate you because I hate loving you. I love you but I don't like you. I hate loving what I don't like. I hate hating you. I wish I could stop hating you and start loving loving you. I am afraid of you. You make me sick. You make my heart beat with a deep quiet-ness that I know to be peace.

Why? Continuum of urban disconnect, why? When the sun rises you will wake me up from my insomnia and refuel me with your frenzy. I flee into the deep.

Musician's Morning

...

EARLY IN THE morning Anosike practised the minor chords on his box guitar, his best friend, whom he called Freedom. His soul was full and empty. He gripped the strings with his heart and gradually played, first arpeggio-style, then a-strumming, slowly changing from one chord to the other, one key to the higher.

Each time he caused the strings to vibrate, each time there arose sound from the instrument, a breath of calm seemed to sink into his soul. He did not want to stop.

By the time it began to grow bright outside, he had gone through only a third of the exercise. With a sigh he dropped Freedom lightly on his sparse, rough bed and arose.

For a few moments he remained motionless on his feet. His chest rose and fell, lightly. A look of gentle, dreamy reflection was trapped upon his face, a hard, rocky face with full lips and a strong, pugnacious forehead. He had an angular skull, radiated an intense and awkward, almost overpowering crude hand-someness. His observant grey-black eyes were turned inwards, his profile was angled towards the window.

It dawned on him again, like it did every once in a while, that destiny is like a skin. It wrapped itself around you even ere you arrived. It encapsules, en-closes, protects and undermines you. Captures you. Teleguides you. It limits you. It links you to your world. It is hard to shed and hard to change. It lasts a lifetime.

Once again a wry smile was his reaction to this ever-recurring moment of recognition. A wry and sad smile. Yet it was a smile of amusement. No wonder snakes shed their skin. His humour was sometimes dark, sometimes light. He suddenly remembered that he had written something into his diary sometime in the middle of the night, something about train tracks, cocoon and the birth of butterfly. He remembered the feeling of the struggling butterfly. He reached across his bed, lifted his diary, opened it and read it again. Everything came back, the nocturnal stab of clarity that subsequent sleep had temporarily blotted out.

It was the same recognition that had just come back again in the skin analogy. Now he felt calmer.

He emerged, composed, out of his reflection and went into the bathroom. A normal prelude to another abnormal day.

This was how it always started – with music, unfinished, and a startling recognition that would fill him all day long. This was the cycle of his life.

An awakening musician.

Your Number

...

WHAT ARE YOU thinking about at this very moment?

It is hardest to know yourself. Before you know yourself you will first come to know many other people. And when it is time to know yourself, you will not see or discover yourself by yourself, but somebody else will show you yourself.

Then you will really know yourself as you are.

If I told you how this train of thought was set off in my mind, you might find it strange, but I learn from little things and I let the little things show me the big things. Big things expose themselves in little things.

It was my mobile phone. My first. I have had it for almost a year now and I use it several times everyday.

My little handy. But I never succeeded in memorising the number. I have seen this number several times, having stored it myself on my phone's own address book, and I have read it out many times to many people. But I have never memorised it.

No, the problem is not with my memory. I *have* other people's landline and mobile numbers in my head. I can reel them all off anytime. But to give you my number I would have had to, even until yesterday evening, look it up first in my address book. *For the umpteenth time!* Even after almost a year.

Yesterday a friend pointed his phone at me and said, What's your number? Oh stop, I have it here, don't I?...

And he thumbed his handset severally and said 08037220738...?

Even before he finished I spoke the last four digits with him, mouthing them at half-volume zero seven three eight...

It was my number. Painted before my mind's eye, recognised instantly by an internal antennae, consciously reactivated. Suddenly it awoke within me like youth awakening into manhood and remembering the code stored within its soul even before birth. Like memory returning of an old book for long forgotten. Now it's at the tips of my fingers, re-echoing in the hallrooms of my head.

I know it off the top of my head. No, I *know* it now.

How? Somebody told it to me. Gave it back to me. It came home, for good. It stuck. His voice. The words. Visual digits. Awakening. Recognition. My own is now mine. For it has come back to me.

Earlier, when I told him about my life, he sat up straight and, pinning me with an incredulous look, said, Man, you have some wild stories to tell.

In my mind I thought, Yes, to tell one day. You haven't heard anything yet. We all have the same thing, and then I've got something more.

The day is dawning well today. The sun is not too bright. I *couldn't* stand that just now.

What do you know about yourself? Your father told you your name. Your country preset your status. The world showed you your race. Society put you in your place. A stranger read your mind. Your lover undid your heart. Your superior told you your job. And the owners of your ear have pointed out to you your style.

In the midst of all this, you want something. But by the time you figure out what it is, you've probably become something else already. Your hopes you exchange for regret. Don't be bitter. Could be worse. Might be better, if you laugh. Truth is, you have never stopped being yourself, the same person I always knew, through it all. We are now even as we were then, at our beginning. But do you remember?

Curriculum Vitae

...

I SIT upon my couch and wonder what to write about, what to lie about.

My CV. What on earth am I going to write on it? Certainly not the truth! You don't land the job by telling the truth. You get it by evading the truth. Retaining just enough of it to escape the justified accusation of deliberate falsification.

So I write.

Name: Udo, Jeremiah Anosike. No, that's too much. Just: *Udo, Jeremiah*.

That's close, pretty close, to it. That way they'll never know who I am. They'll have, however, a voiceable sound with which to refer to me. An urban approximation, the result of western colonisation and foreign religion. I think I will enjoy this game, of using my own self as my camouflage. I can hardly contain my laughter.

Slowly they begin to see me, to know me. What's your name? Jeremiah Udo. Call me Jerry, or Miah. Call me Miah. Everyone calls me Miah. Nice to meet you, Miah. *Miah?* From where? You mean, where I come from or where I'm coming from? – No, stop, wrong reply – Answer: From here. Yes, from here. Good Answer! Here. Where's here? Who cares. Hey guys, meet Miah. He's from here too. Cool, nice to meet you. Catch ya later.

I was born, like everyone else, alone. What I like most when I look out the window are green plants, some sprouting from the ground, some growing in pots, some clinging to trees or walls, or hanging down upsideup.

Were a day to pass by without my seeing them, how would I go on? All these shades of green. All this nature. God's Work.

I once used to know an artist. Actually he was a sculptor, he sculpted with wood. I mean, he was an artist.

A good fellow, brown as wood and green as leaves. A hardy, earthy, earthen character and a depth as soulful as a wishing well.

I wish him well...

We did not grow up together. We met after we had

grown up and together we grew back into children.

The second child is the wiser here.

Whenever he gripped with his hands a piece of wood and set his knife to it, his shoulders broad, his eyes brooding, his eyes at peace, I am happy we met.

I write this story for him. If you look carefully, you will see that I write in the second hand and not in the first. The first went with him.

Words, of late, tire me.

Certainly I could have prevented his death, of that I am certain. But his death prevented me.

The little things I cannot write about – the swinging twine, swaying in the evening breeze, hanging down from the banana tree –

I am inside, you are outside. Lie. You are inside. I am outside.

The uncountable leaves, each with a design of its own, differently carved, differently coloured with its own green and changing green.

Are you so many? Are you not one? Are all these you? All these thoughts and thoughts of you. You grow, you branch out, more and more everyday.

Your kindness undid you. A profusion of ever flourishing and emerging leaves, emergent, that was your kindness.

And even as they fade away, they come again.

I remember the reclining chair you carved.

I sat on it and felt the strong fingers of your steady

hand encapsule me, gently, gently, I had no fear.

The little wooden combs you carved. They line the window, a prelude to the world without, the world within, brown and green, and deeply through the greenery, an understanding of blue. You combed their hearts all through.

I bring that world into my house, like the second gas equation was dragged into the first, and I arrive at an unfaltering constancy. The world is constant.

Friends float away. They forget the poems they shared and the light they saw, a step away.

They stepped aside.

Sometimes I remember. Sometimes.

I only remember when I remember. Else I know not that I forgot. I'm filled only with a strange sorrow, and I know that something is gone. But what?
It can't be just you. These final memories.

Why on earth did you join the demonstration? I told you not to, not to believe these promisers of change. But you told me this was our time and this was our calling and all the rest of that jargon which I now wish I had never put into your mind in the first place when we first met. I really should learn to hold my tongue. Well, the price of fuel was slightly brought back down again, finally. The union had a closed door meeting with the government and the 'industry stakeholders', and then the strike was called off.

The soldier who pulled the trigger was never identified. People have gone on with their lives. There were a few newspaper articles about your 'martyrical' (who comes up with such words?) death, but other news have sort of replaced you now. But don't worry, I'll correct that some day, hero. What still hurts me the most is that someone took your watch off your wrist before I got to you. Remember that watch? We bought two of them, an identical pair, at the same time, one for you and one for me. Now it feels like I'm just here, marking time. My hero is gone.

There are rumours that the price of fuel will be raised again before the end of the year. Should I join the protest, wear a t-shirt with your face printed on it? How many soldiers and policemen on the bulleting this time before they hold the next closed door meeting?

Let's talk of other things, undying things.

Apropos:

Once it rained so heavily that the roofs began to leak. Only then did we realise the limitations of our roof. Who repaired it? Was it you or I?

Sculptor, sculptor, you or I?

I wish I were a sculptor: so I could sculpt all those pieces you described to me, pieces you planned to sculpt, if you had not died.

Who died? I think it was I. Died when I started believing you had died. Who died?

My heart is heavy, I will not lie, I need a break –

I've had my break, my big break, but I refused to break. Break even.

I'm not like you. I have to suffer, I know not why. Nobody likes the things I write, it seems. In the second hand. My hand. Not like you. But I know what you would say to me, like always: *You write for the deep, so don't expect accolade on the surface; it would be an insult; and I would have nothing to inspire me.* The seriousness in your eyes was my greatest reward, each time you spoke.

They loved your sculptures, they bought them and took them home with them into their homes. Can you imagine that? Do you remember? Into their homes. They will always love you. Never ask me again if I am jealous of you.

The keys are lying on the table. This is the moment. The almighty present. Still I write in the second hand.

Am I denying myself? Am I living a lie? Whose lie? Your lie? You had your lies too. You lied too.

But is the night not the day's lie? And what a beautiful lie, full of mystery. A deep lie, above all. Because, actually, there is always light in the centre.

The stronger the sound, the louder the echo. Live well, dear friend, live well.

Before the sun tells another lie, before the day gives way to night, before we part let's meet again, you and I.

The house is cool tonight. Cool and quiet. It's taken

me a long time and a hard struggle to get here, far from my goal. I would have arrived here sooner if I had not listened to her. But you told me to listen to her and she sent me down the wrong lane.

There I lost everything, including myself. So I guess in the end it was worth it. And it's all because of you. You carved this out too. You were a carver too.

There is no knock on the door tonight. She's gone away. The phone will not ring, my postbox shall stay empty, I will not receive any email or text message.

All I'll ever have is what I have. All I want is this: The ability to move on. One day, I know, I'll find the real one.

When the sun was setting on the picture of the thoughtful woman, you said:

Mm mm mm.

Sweet delight.

Recently I thought of you again. The thought hurt me. I wished you were around. I rarely do so, because it doesn't matter. But this time it did, this time I did. Wishing it made me stronger. I knew you for less than a year. I *knew* you.

The way you walk, the way you work. The way you pause and consider the cut, the last cut and the one approaching your hand. You cut.

You carve.

You sculpt. Woodcarver. Woodsculptor. Stonewood. Artist. Art *ist Art. Gleichart.*

This by the way is a new day. Something like a new page in an unending old book. They call it a new leaf. Green leaf swelling.

The leaves are still new outside. They are not overly loud now. The sun sinks. Night falls. For some reason I suddenly remember the story you told me about your crazy grandfather, or was it greatgrandfather, living alone on some wild hill somewhere in your village. I almos envy him now.

The thought that crossed my mind is almost gone. Yes. The thought of you. But the deepinnerfeelings remain where they always were before they were sounded by an ever returning thought, a comet, it will recur, re-occur. You, my star.

There was a time when I did not know you. There was a time when I could not have known you. Then we met. That day on the street. On the road. The road. Now I'm struggling on without you. You were my friend. I met you at the end, the sweetest time to meet. The hardest time to part. There is nothing so traumatic as the end. Never meet at the end, nor part ever there too. Whatever you want to do, do it in the beginning; be it meeting or parting, uniting or departing or working together, do it in the beginning if you cannot bear the pain.

But if you can bear the pain, and if you love life like I do, then do it also at the end. Then will it change your life. I love, above all, the end. For there is none.

It was short, our time. Our song. Is this truly the end? Our end of the rainbow.

Your carvings surround me everywhere. The chair on which I sit was carved by you, I call it my couch. How then do I forget you? The table on which I write was carved by you – there is none better – how then could I forget you?

Your style whiles away my loneliness.

Your works sell well. What should I do with the money? I don't want to squander it on day-to-day survival.

I want to use it for something great. That's why I'm applying for this job. It's an oil company, by the way. Yes I know, I can almost hear your horrified voice: *Et tu, Brute?* But please forgive me. I know it might look like treachery, but I really really need the dough. I want to make my own money. Then I can use yours to do something you always wanted. It has to do with her. She's okay, really. I just didn't understand her really.

Don't laugh, I'm serious.

What on earth should I write on my CV.? I have no idea, I don't know where to start, it's all too much. My life feels like an old book, forever unfinished, whose chapters keep on changing, whose pages keep on rewriting and redefining themselves as ever new ones appear. I think I'll just keep it simple. Very simple. I'll tell them the name on my birth certificate. I won't even tell them my name, the one you gave me. I'll tell them the date on my birth certificate, but I won't tell them the day I was born, the day we awakened the real in one another, our birthday, my most recent history.

I'll tell them the schools and institutions I attended, the subjects and courses I did there. But I won't tell them the things you and I discovered. The real things. I'll tell them the places I've worked. But I won't tell them the things we worked at. I'll never tell them all that we worked at. Those are ours alone. You and I.

Yes, I'll only tell them lies, the world's global superficial lies. The lies that make up our lives. That's what I'll write into my CV. The truth I'll keep to us. In my first hand.

It will follow me to the grave, and rise one day with me to there where you, hopefully, already are.

Awaken, My Flower

...

ONCE UPON A time, here beside your heart, I waited. I waited and waited, but you did not open up. Why? I thought you said you loved me. Finally I knocked on the door, but the door did not open up. So I knocked on the window, but the window remained shut. Then I peered in through the glass-pane of the window. The curtains were drawn aside, I had a clear view into your heart.

You were lying on a couch, a soft couch, you were sleeping. What were you dreaming of? I did not know. Whom were you dreaming of? I did not know. Your eyes were closed, just like your door and your window, there was a peaceful look on your face.

You looked so restful that I did not want to disturb

you. I would gladly have remained outside rather than disturb the serene sleep of your heart. But, you see, it's cold outside and it's getting dark, and strange figures approach me and call me by strange names to which I know that I must never answer or I'll be caught and I'll be dead.

Won't you open up the door? Won't you awaken from your sleep?

So I began to sing. It was a song that I had never sung before, a new song that arose unbidden from my heart. The song entered into your sleep and entered into your dream and showed you the way out of your subconsciousness, and led you out of the hall of dreams... and, as your eyes opened, you saw me at the window and I saw the love and the fear in your eyes. Love because you love me. Fear because the monster is standing over me.

But if you rush to the door on time and open it quickly, I will escape the monster and you and I will become one heart.

Hurry up, dear, I'm almost dead.

The Old Poet

...

THE OLD poet stood silently upon the highest peak of the Jos plateau and sensed, for the first time in his long life, that it was time to finally put into words the yearnings, the stirrings and the recognitions that had ravaged his heart through the course of his life's wanderings.

His eyes were raised to the sky, but he saw sky not, nor cloud, nor bird, nay, nor sun, for he was blind. As blind as blind can be. So who shall write down his poems on his behalf? – With a heavy heart he descended the Shere hills, his faithful brown mongrel, leashed, leading him into the valley.

It was two long unbearable weeks later that he encountered Bingel, a young boy, stout of body and heart and perpetually serious, strolling, eyes hooded, in these savannah fields. He stopped. He stopped too:

"I see you not, yet know I that you but a child still are: Your step, though slow, is untempered... your breathing, though measured, is free. Yes, though I see not, indeed I know that though you be young, at heart are you a man; for your step, though untempered, is slow, and your breathing, though free, is measured."

The young wanderer looked at this old poet who said things he almost understood.

"And what do you want from me?" queried Bingel.

"Once I was a youth like you, wandering through these very same fields, pondering true over those very same questions that course right now through your heart! The answers I found, I did not under-stand; the answers I would have understood, I did not find. Thus had I to journey through life, learning through experiencing, finding not by thinking but by acting. And now that I, aged and blinded by life, stand before you today, it is with the ironic recognition that I have learnt nothing new in my old age which I did not already silently know in my youth, but now the knowledge I have, I understand, because the knowl-edge I would understand, I have. And yet the strange gap remains: I am still not complete.

"Above that, a certain peace eludes me still for I yet must ink into readable words the river of thoughts flowing in my soul; but how can a blind man write when he cannot see what he once could see when he could not write? Thus has destiny brought you to me today, my friend, to be my hand and to be my eyes, to write down on my behalf what I shall dictate to you, all I have to give, which is nought but that already in your own ancient heart, my son! This might sound strange to you now, but I am the answer you came here seeking today, for there are no accidents in life."

Now the youth Bingel gazed long and hard, long at the old poet and hard at the ground, and then slowly began to speak:

"I fathom not one word which you have spoken, yes, not one. And since you say that all you know, already I know too, and yet I experience thus that I understand not what you say, then truly you have erred and I am not the one you seek! A blind man cannot see and so *cannot see me!* I cannot write down words which are alien to me and which will perhaps render me just as blind as you are, hobbling askance in lonely fields day and night, speaking double-sided words unconstruable to all but you."

And so saying, the young philosopher walked off and walked away, the tremulous pleas of the old poet dying away unheeded behind his upright retreating form.

The blind old poet found no-one to write down his heart's poems on his behalf and, just as he had lived with them, died with them veiled, untilled, still deep within his lonely heart.

The young boy grew up, still trying to understand those same strange, vague longings that took him into those lonely savannah fields in his youth. However, like the old poet, he found answers which were no answers, but only newer questions. And so, just like the oldman-poet, he experienced a very turbulent earthlife - one in which violence, bigotry and lack of understanding among the peoples grew from genera-tion to generation. A life which, by its end, had made a poet of Bingel and rendered him blind too – full of the urge to write in words the poems weighing bright in his heart, but hoping for a willing hand to be his needed tool.

This morning he stood upon the very same peak on which, eighty years ago, the old poet had once also stood, and understood the very same strange and simple things the old poet had once grasped, for he had also become a blind old poet. For him too, the gaps remain and he is conscious of his incompletion.

Slowly he descended the Shere hills of the Jos pla-teau with his dog, his only companion; silvery tears glistened in his sightless eyes as he painfully remem-bered a friend he met, decades ago, on these very same rustic, primeval planes.

And so did I meet him, broken, upon his knees, blinded and in tears – *the old poet*. I stopped... And then made to continue, but he held me with his trembling old hand. And...

"What do you want from me!?" I demanded.

Gently Bingel began:

"Once I was a youth like you, wandering through these very same fields, pondering true over those very same questions that course right now through your heart! *The answers I found, I did not understand...*"

Hard To Grasp

...

ONCE UPON a time, a man woke up and gazed upon a thought hanging in the air above his bed.

And the longer he looked at it, the more it confused him. And when he looked away, he forgot it.

Through the day it disturbed him, a memory he was trying to remember, but could not remember what he was trying to remember. But this he remembered: I am not who I think I am.

So this thought – I am not who I think I am – stayed with him for many hours, each as long as a decade, as he tried to fathom its meaning. Verily, it became his very name. His very aim.

Many hearts. In which one lies the answer? So he broke them open and left them behind, ravaged, the sought unfound.

He is written about in the books of men. His character has been copied and reproduced in stories down the ages – the raging, ravaging beast that consumes hearts and upturns nations. In truth he is a tireless seeker, and always giving. In shrouded truth. Love and peace cloaked in battle and tears. Shredding hearts to pieces with merciless thirst. How many times has he altered history, chasing the mirror? Thus has his troublesome picture been painted before him repeatedly. Thus too does he see himself, hours later.

But all I want is to find the key. Burning Flame, you are not who you THINK you are. This thought nags in him. Remember.

I am a warrior. No.

I am a lover. No.

You are a bridge. Just be.

Just be.

There! There it is again, the morning-thought, hanging once more in the sky above his mind. Hard to grasp:

Just be.

The Bridge Across The River

...

THERE IS a bridge across the River Niger. A cold, old steel bridge across the long-travelling river. It is to this busy bridge that once the painter came every-day, every evening – oblivious, as one drugged, to the noise of the hawkers around, and the cars behind, her – as she stared into the hurrying water, and tried to exchange her sorrow for joy.

Unfortunately she was rarely ever able to achieve this, but just as she had come with her sorrow, she would depart with it as well.

Life is especially uncomfortable for artists, living as they do in their two worlds – the tangible world we normal people see and the other, invisible, one seemingly perceivable only by the inner eyes of artists. They cannot help it. It is their destiny, their perpetual calling, their fate. It seems as though the Divine has assigned to them the painful task of bridging for mankind groping blindfolded on earth the gap of the river of sightlessness which flows between that which was, that which is and that which will be, the perceived and unseen. This, they say, is why artists suffer, torn in different directions by irrenconciliable forces.

Ijeoma the painter had had quite a happy childhood on the other side of the river, in a small town called Obosi. She played with her brothers and sisters and was all but completely unconscious of the adult life around her. Her most insistent love manifested itself in the urge to gaze upon pictures – in books or in nature or even upon the faces of her fellow human beings. To paint however she had never attempted, never contemplated. Neither the urge nor the idea had ever occurred to her.

Until she became an adolescent and the strange, irresistible longing and pain gripped her and forced her to spread out upon plain, empty waiting sheets the pictures of the secret knowledge which she found that she already, unaccountably, bore inside her mysterious soul. And she painted...

Painting made Ijeoma happy. Gave her release and, simultaneously, gripped her inexorably. A caged, sky-free bird. The bane of artists, their incentive, their riddle, their sorrow, their reward.

But then she fathomed the world no more. And in return the world fathomed her no more too, gradually proceeding to pin such labels upon her as *queer... funny... disturbed... unbalanced... mad.* She however, she knew that those labels fit not her but the world which sought to stick them on her. Like they also say, in the society of mad people, the sane one becomes crazy.

Ijeoma drew away from people and drew herself into art. Loneliness became her companion. She tried to understand herself. Was her heart a running stream that flowed into the sea? Was her heart a sky upon which angels had painted since forever? Or was it a universe, a meeting place of forces, a tended garden, blended carefully? Or just another ordinary human heart?

Then arrived the time in which she had to begin to fend for herself, for as childhood becomes youth, so becomes youth adulthood. And adulthood must hold its head high, and be self-dependent.

She had learned no other trade but the trade of images, illustrated moods and pictures. So she began to frame and sell her paintings. But nobody bought them; nobody bought these paintings which one day in the future would suddenly become masterpieces. But artists, who see well humanity's future, are notoriously incapable of seeing their own.

Life became to Ijeoma like an empty desert. If she could eat once a day, she was lucky. She moved to the other side of the river, to a town called Asaba where she lived alone, away from home. But somebody once said that home is inside.

Her family, although they did not understand her, continued to write to her every now and then however, as families like to do. And to offer help, *if...*

She did not always reply, as offsprings and artists are wont to do. But whenever she did she never dwelled upon the fact of her poor financial and living conditions, but deliberately insisted she was fine. Ijeoma sent home tiny pretty parcels every once in a while, parcels she had bought with her few small savings, not because she wanted to buy them, but because her pride would not let her project any other but this picture of herself to those from whom she wanted no pity.

And then things came to a peak. In order to be able to hang on, it turned out that she would have to open her heart to the well-meant charity of a certain man who had met her and who could not help but love her with his whole wide soul.

It was not that she did not want to, or that she felt it would be wrong to do so with regards to this particular man in whose eyes she saw distant, radiant things that made her heart jump, for then her compulsive resistance would have been understandable. It was just that she did not want to let go of her tenacious pride.

She was sad, angry, bewildered and embittered by the fact that her paintings were not loved, sought after, bought. It hurt her deep within her soul.

She took to visiting the bridge across the river every evening, standing on its central spot and staring into the non-chalant waters, like many lonely people do.

And one day as she stood there, under a humid sun, a lurid idea with which she had long toyed gripped her anew with near ineludible force.

Her head swam, she became dizzy. She was aware of herself toppling over the railing into the river of blindness, but she made no effort to arrest her fall; silently she gave herself up to that fate which she had decided would be hers. The water rushed up fast.

She fell voluntarily into the river and drowned and died so that everything would at last come to an end...

And this is where the story begins. I have spoken to many a native who hawks upon this bridge or casts the net from his fishing boat into the waters of River Niger, and they all swear that this is true.

Ijeoma was very surprised, after she dumped herself into the river, to experience that everything did not come to an end. Although her body died, she herself continued to drown in the watching water, drown but not die, *drown and yet not die,* unremittingly.

Meanwhile Okeke, that man with the distant, radiant things in his eyes who loved her more than he had ever believed one human being could love another, came to look for her at the old bridge, her bridge of sighs, seized of a sudden and inexplicable apprehension. Amidst the agitation of the crowd that had gathered on the bridge, pointing in consternation into the river, he saw her scarf hanging from the railing, but her he saw no more...

Decades later, Ijeoma watches an old man emerge from a parked car by the side of the road and slowly limp his way up the bridge. The hawkers, peddling everything from smart phones to impotency-curing ointments, seem to know him well, they make way for him. He takes no notice of them, or of the hustle and bustle of traffic and trade, the stench of sweat and exhaust fumes. In one hand he holds a scarf, faded yellow, with his other hand he rubs his tired old eyes wearily. Finally he gets to where Ijeoma is standing, in the middle of the bridge, peers briefly at her with a confused, introspective look in his eyes, blinks, then turns and stares quietly down into the river.

Standing beside him, she watches him, says nothing, so as not to disturb the solemnity of this ever-recurring magic moment. She drinks in the love that emanates like waves with his thoughts. After a while, he lets out a soft long sigh, straightens up, rubs his thigh where the old shrapnel is still embedded, and looks at the sky. This is her cue; she decides to try again. Taking a deep breath, she raises her hand, places it on his shoulder and says gently:

"Okeke..."

He does not stir, does not react.

She shakes his shoulder again, and again; her voice is laced with resignation as she utters his name. She knows he will not hear, yet she can't help but try. Each time. Each evening. The same words...

"Okeke... thank you... but move on. My burden is mine alone to bear... to make good."

... she reads in his thoughts that the few finished works she left behind on earth are now masterpieces. In his heart she sees his memories of a proud and beautiful eighteen year old lady from decades ago when he was just a young eager man of twenty.

Before he walks away, he looks at the river again, an introspective, philosophic look on his face, softening the longing in his eyes. As always the last thing he does before he goes is to whisper her name...

"Ijeoma..." *Safe journey.*

Then he turns and limps away, a phlegmatic old man. With tears in her eyes, she watches him walk away, wants to follow, to try one more time. In vain she looks around again for the invisible chain that holds her to this spot, this spot to which she has cumbersomely dragged herself after decades of struggle, of laboriously climbing out of the water and struggling up the bridge.

They have been decades of cavernous emotion. Unnoticed by any, she watched the civil war that brought down the old bridge and catapulted the souls of the many massacred out of the realm of flesh and bone. She was there when the bridge was rebuilt and the war survivors, walking reservoirs of devastated trust and defiant hope, slowly repopulated the bridge.

And still, the longing to fulfil her art burns in her heart. Often has she tried to turn around and return to some distant luminous home... but she cannot. She is held here as by an invisible chain. Destiny unfulfilled, she must cross the bridge again, one day.

And soon she will be born anew into the earth as a baby. She will grow into a deep dreamy teenager and then mature into a restless and intense artist. Perhaps she will cross your path. Attract you with her art, intrigue you with her nature and remain incomprehensible. If she does, do meet her with understanding. She is a bridge. She paints for you and me.

Two Paintings

...

A YOUNG MAN. Alone. Poverty-stricken. What shall he do to survive? He has only one talent, much un-used: he can draw and paint. He had done it all his short life, since that moment when he first saw the paintings of that legendary artist who killed herself as a young woman, long ago in the old Nigeria, be-fore the war. Her paintings seemed to have torn open wounds within his heart from which, ceaselessly, it gushed forth.

Growing up in the mad heady dash to afro-moder-nity that was Lagos, he had forgotten to back himself up with an alternative education while following with audacious self-will his crazy passion and living his dream. Now he stood on the brink of starvation and understood her. But he also knew that if he had armed himself with an alternative, he would today in hungry desperation betray everything he believed in, and he was glad he had not. For this one thing he knew: he would never give up. One day, the tables would turn. So the struggle continued. And then one day arrived in which he had absolutely nothing left and knew not what to do.

Finally he mixed his last paints and, full of anguish, loneliness and a something else not easy to define, wrought two paintings upon two round, flat surfaces, and stood with them beside a mechanic workshop on one of the busy roadsides in Lagos, to peddle them, and eat.

A woman passing in a car beheld the two paintings and the hawker. In Nigeria, people hawk any and all things which they can lay their hands on. Therefore, the woman never even gave thought to the notion that that ragged bony pauper might have actually painted those works himself. All she knew, straightaway, was that they were masterpieces. So she stopped and bargained them down to a cruelly small price and bought them off him, believing in her mind that he must have stolen them from somewhere, thus whatever amount he sold them for would still mean a profit. She bought them for the price of a day's meal.

But as she was driving away she chanced to glance

into the rear-view mirror and noticed the hawker still standing there, gazing after her with a strange, intense, burning look on his face. Suddenly she just knew that he was the artist, the painter who executed these works personally.

She began to do a u-turn but before she was done a sportscar had gone out of control and hit the dreaming painter and sped off. He was on the brink of no return by the time she got to him, and then, after exchanging a look of unwordable intimacy with her, he died, in her arms, his two eyes open, still looking at her.

And suddenly she wondered why he looked so strongly familiar.

She hung his two paintings in her home, for she felt an irresistible connection to these her only connections to that unknown pauper. There was something about the paintings...

One was about women bathing in a stream...

The other was about women lying dead in the woods...

In both paintings, outside the woods, was a single gravestone, with an old woman standing beside it, looking towards the woods with a worried expression on her wise old face.

The paintings held her like a spell.

One day, another woman, one with whom she was bound by quarrels and disagreements and tensions, came calling on her for the purpose of continuing an old line of altercation and settling an old debt. She was one of her bitterest foes.

But then her eyes fell upon, she saw and fell in love with the two paintings, this other woman too. Her heart fell upon them. When the first woman still proved unable to pay back the huge financial debt she owed her, she asked for one of the paintings instead. With anguished heart, the first lady surrendered one, the one where the women lay dead in the woods.

Her foe took it away and hung it up in her home. A few days later she called to ask after the painter of this work, for it seemed to her so familiar. Together they visited his grave, and, for some reason, bitterly wept.

With time they began to call on each other more often, each wanting to see the other painting and to discuss the effect they had on them. So did their bond become mystic, the two women. Each feels an intense connection to the paintings and, through them, to the unknown artist who wrought them, he who seemed so familiar. Their feud came to an end, replaced by a sense of kinship older and deeper than words could explain.

Two paintings. One artist, dead and buried; but his works live on.

And both women still cannot understand what the two paintings mean, nor why they move them both. They only know that the artist had deposited more than just two masterpieces on earth. Verily, he seemed indeed to have also deposited two mistresses and peace on earth, and then departed. –

ii.

Songs of the Wanderer

...

The Seven Brothers From Sokoto

...

THERE WERE once seven brothers from Sokoto who were in everything contrary. They were of contrary mentality and of contrary belief. And, returning from worship on a Sunday morning to find their family home raided and burned yet again in another stab of religious violence, they finally yielded to the plea of their dying father to leave him there in their ancestral land and move south to a place where they could build safe lives for themselves.

Being contrary as they were, the brothers decided that this was the best opportunity to actualise a dream they had always borne deep within their hearts. They

decided to find the sea. This was a monumental decision, for the desire to get to the sea had long been
the professed desire of many a soul from their corner of the country, for all kinds of different reasons.
Now they decided to find it and get to understand this
mysterious pull. They knelt down solemnly before
the dying Namah, their father, he blessed them with
the sign of the cross; and then after one last tearful
embrace with Awabe, their gracefully ageing mother,
the seven brothers from Sokoto left the large rocky
hills and wide arid plains of their homeland behind
them as they set off to find the sea.

They journeyed for a long time. They passed towns
and villages and towns again, then came one evening to a village which at first seemed to be empty.
Curiously they made their way towards the village
square where they found the entire community sitting around a storyteller. The storyteller was an old
man who in his youth had travlled far and wide, seen
many wonders, survived many adventures and accu-
mulated many memories in his soul. Having arrived,
in his travels, the twilight of his life, he parted gener-
ously with these memories, cloaked as stories, sharing them with grateful listeners who repaid him with
money, clothes, food and, most precious of all, smiles.
His old age thus became too a beautiful experience of
which he would one day tell, cloaked as a new story,
in a new life when he came back to the earth.

The seven brothers from Sokoto were welcomed into the audience and listened to what the storyteller had to say today. Was it providence? For upon this special evening, the old storyteller was telling the village folk about the sea, the immeasurably great sea at the other end of this large country. Magnificent was the sea, he said, and powerful, surging like the roaring of angry giants.

The diminutive, bald-headed chronicler sighed, looked far into the distance of his memory, and added in his surprisingly strong voice that the sea was close to indescribable. It needed to be seen in order to be understood, believed. It was vast, vaster then minds could grasp, and at its outermost boundary, far beyond reach, shone the line of God's light.

Nor was the sea empty. It was bordered by strange hollow stones called sea-shells and populated with creatures of all types and sizes – he tried to describe fish ten times as large as human beings, and multiple-limbed creatures, and beastial hunters more ferocious than lions. The pictures he painted were gripping. In colourful language he tried and tried to describe the character of the sea, in perpetual motion, never still, water coming and going forever, rocking back and forth.

The listeners were mesmerized. What kind of water was this?

But that was not all, said the wizened old storyteller; there was more, much more to be said about the sea, but it was getting late... he would continue the story the next day. With great effort he stood up, his folded skin, stubborn like old brown leather, reluctantly stretching into its imitation of an upright form. The people were disappointed, they groaned, yet nobody complained. They all loved the storyteller and followed him at his pace.

The seven brothers prepared to travel on before the sun set completely. But Kerma, the first of the seven, was suddenly seized by a contrary ambition. He was a student, a learner, by nature, and had been gripped the deepest by the words of the storyteller. Solemnly Kerma announced to his brothers that he was going to stay here with these villagers and listen to this glorious storyteller who unveiled the sea to him. He could not understand why the others were travelling on. Did they not know that here they would realise their longing of finding the sea?

Nothing that any of the others told him could make him change his mind. Bluntly Kerma blocked his ears to their words and maintained his stand: *Here he had found the sea!*

So his six brothers turned their eyes to the road and sojourned on, hungry for the sea, their appetite whetted by the storyteller's tales. Further south they travelled, seeking the sea. They crossed boundaries and hills and then one day they came upon a mighty river, the grand River Niger!

How were they going to cross it? They thought and searched, but saw neither boat nor bridge. They then set off down the banks of the river until finally they saw some of the inhabitants of a rustic little village. To them they revealed their mission, explained their present predicament – they did not know how to cross the river.

There were indeed a few bridges across the river, answered the very curious villagers, but they were few and far between. The next one was further yet down the river. Together they all walked along until they got there. As they were then about to cross the bridge, taking their departure from the helpful villagers, whom they had however also paid for their services, one of the villagers mentioned in passing that this river actually eventually flowed into the sea.

Into the sea?, cried Bandi, the second of the seven brothers.

Yes, the villagers said.

Bandi was a true adventurer by nature. Having understood that this river flowed into the sea, he made the decision to buy a boat and navigate the flowing river to its end, the sea. This he revealed to his brothers.

They reflected upon his words individually. His ambition made sense. And yet...! – they had set off to find *the sea*, and by *walking south* they would arrive at the sea. This here was a river, not the sea; nor were they trained mariners.

They bade their restless brother farewell and continued towards the sea. Let Bandi be content in his belief that in the river lay his possibility of finding the sea. Every man has his free will, let each man be free.

The remaining five brothers journeyed on. On their path they met many a city, each full of attractions new and interesting. Unable to resist the temptation to explore, they lingered a little in each new place before they moved on. It was not long before they, upon entering a certain city, found themselves in a marketplace of arts and craft. There they came across a group of people admiring a giant-sized painting... a painting of the sea!

The five brothers halted in wonder and gazed at this beautiful painting of such extraordinary beauty. This was their first time of ever seeing the sea, albeit a painting of it. The sight stunned them! It seemed as if they were standing at a mighty window, gazing out into eternity. And as they stared at it in awe and wonder, the third of the seven made his own decision.

Azeka was a quiet person, he did not talk much. Opening his wallet, he extracted the exact amount of money demanded and bought the masterpiece. When his brothers asked him what he was doing, he told them that with this painting his ambition had been fulfilled. *How glorious... could they not see it?*

They could not. Silently shaking his head to himself, Azeka walked away from them to build a quiet house for himself away from crowds, and hung his painting on the wall where he could see it everyday. Now he would forever have the sea with him. For the quiet, introspective Azeka, the painting was the sea.

Four brothers were left. They progressed on, further south. The vegetation, climate, landscape changed as they plunged deeper into the tropics.

Eventually they got into the city that was the gateway to the last western stretch of the south, leading to the sea. Soon they came upon a place they learned to be something called a club. The name plastered upon it was what arrested their attention – "Big Sea!"

They stopped, their eyes thoughtful, and looked in. It was a recreational establishment with a very large swimming pool in which many children and adults swam and made a lot of noise. The most impressive thing about this water was that, for some strange reason, it was actually in motion, rocking back and forth the whole time, like the storyteller had once described. How was that possible? Was this the sea?

For the first time, all four brothers were confused. Then the fourth, Diri, a somewhat physically fragile, but fun-loving and sociable character, wearied from the long march across the land, suddenly made his decision. *Yes, this was the sea!*

Buying a pair of swim trunks, Diri happily jumped in and joined the people playing in the pool.

The last three brothers, however, remained doubtful that this was the sea, however much like the sea it looked, and silently they journeyed on... until they arrived at a land of which they soon learned that it bordered the sea, and which called itself a land of aquatic spleandour.

It was not long and they began to intermittently happen upon strange hollow stones which they were told were sea shells. Lots and lots of them. And laughing triumphantly, Senchi, the fifth of the seven, a brilliant-minded man full of scientific curiousity, picked up the shells and began to study them, declaring:

"Look! I have found the sea."

Without saying any further word to his brothers, he walked away, picking shells.

Had Senchi gone mad?

His brothers could not wait to find out... the sea was too close. They left him and hurried ahead.

Now there were only two left. They walked and walked, walked and walked, tirelessly. Finally they got to the edge of the mainland and gazed across the lagoon at the island. Or rather, the seventh gazed across the lagoon. The sixth only gazed at the lagoon.

Chonoko's senses swirled. Joy erupted within him like a volcano. He could smell the ocean very strongly... he saw shells everywhere... he felt the soft sand... marveled at the sight of the lagoon, water everywhere... and he began to weep with deep emotion. Were these not the promised signs?

After *all* these months of travelling, *at last* he had found the sea. Gratitude welled up in him, gratitude to God. Chonoko, a deeply religious fellow, sank down to his knees and in a trembling whisper uttered words and songs of praise to his faithful God. Then, full of a mixture of trepidation and excitement, he dived into the lagoon and happily began to splash about.

But the seventh... he looked at his brother for a long time and he looked at the lagoon. Everything seemed so right. Then his eyes arose and he gazed in quiet curiousity at the little bridge that stretched over the lagoon, from the mainland to the island...

What if?...

And quietly Peni began to climb the bridge, and he walked across the lagoon and stepped upon the island.

Gradually he progressed.

As Peni moved forward, his thoughts travelled backwards in time, back to his arid northern homeland of many trees and few rivers, the thick bushes that crowded around his father's household well. He remembered the mixed emotions with which the seven brothers impressed upon their memory for the last time the old faces of Namah and Awabe, their father and mother, as they took their leave. He remembered their determination to find the sea, the cameraderie which had united them as they set forth upon their way. And he remembered his six brothers who were now no longer with him:

The first, the knowledge-hungry Kerma, who joined the listeners of a story...; the second, the wild and adventurous Bandi, who began to sail a river...; the third, the dreamy introspective Azeka, who bought a man-made painting...; the fourth, the fun-loving Diri, who joined sunny pool-swimmers...; the fifth, the brilliant man of science Senchi, who started picking shells...; the sixth, the gratefully believing and religious Chonoko, who dived into a lagoon... -

And he the seventh, Peni, he knew there was, there *must be*, something more. So he kept on walking. He stopped not, looked neither left nor right, just kept on walking... walking... walking...

On and on.

First he heard the roar... and then, rounding a corner as he emerged from inner streets... suddenly... he saw the Sea.

For a long time Peni stood still, breathless, and looked at it. The sea was glorious, more magnificent in real life than any story or painting could depict, grander than any river or pool.

He breathed out and at once the shock of the attainment of his goal, of the encountering of the sheer size of it, fell away. He inhaled the rough sea wind sharply and let it out again as a cry of joy that pierced crudely the loud shout of the ocean. A silent, wordless prayer of gratitude fortified his heart.

And then Peni put his quivering little boat upon the sea and set sail towards the Horizon.

Metamorphosis

. . .

THERE ONCE LIVED a girl called Vanity. It was in that strange country where newborn babies are left unnamed – simply being referred to as so and so's first son, so and so's third daughter, etc – until they have grown into childhood. Only then would their parents and relatives, having up to this time carefully studied the character (for early dawns day) of the one to be named – finally confer upon the child that name which they believed best captured the essence of its core personality.

And so did this girl, from an early age, come to be called Vanity, for she was as proud and vainglorious as a peacock. Vanity believed that the whole world was there just to serve and admire her. She did not care much for others, nor could she tolerate, in her vicinity, another receiving more attention, admiration and adoration than herself. This she simply could not bear. She thus constantly went to all and any lengths to make sure that the attention of everybody would always and only be riveted upon only her. Vanity dressed in the most beautiful of clothes, wore the most attractive ornaments, learned the most alluring manners of self-expression, perfected the most sensational methods of walking and *swinging*, and – being the scion of wealthy royalty – made it very obvious to the gentry that she had a lot of wealth to spread around. The inevitable consequence of this was that the world divided itself into two groups before her – those who crowded themselves around her and those who avoided her. Great was her pleasure, for 'her side' verily outnumbered the other side.

As she grew into a teenage adolescent, a spectacular beauty happened to grow out upon Vanity's features and fitted itself around her form. Naturally this pleased Vanity extremely and only served to confirm for her and her court her egotistical claim to prenatal supremacy. And at this point her name changed spontaneously from Vanity to Beauty. Beauty became the rave of her time, the talk of town, the object of the envy and idolisation of the women, the desire of the men – exactly what she wanted. Beauty wore her outward beauty like a trophy and used it ruthlessly to acquire everything she wanted, most of which she indeed also got. For people practically worshipped Beauty; they made her their idol, their goddess, their queen. She controlled all.

Such was it that by the time she had become a young woman her name had changed once more – and now everybody called her Power. Power exalted in this name granted to her by her fellow human beings and proceeded to have a crown manufactured for herself on which her name was inscribed for all to see. She became so full of herself that there was no space left for her in which she could continue to expand, nor could her bloated ego grow any further. It neared its peak, its limits. Her ways became stiff and cold, lifeless. She could not find any further height to reach and claim. She became an ornament herself.

And very soon her name became Rigidity. For rigidly fixed was she to the dogged attachment to vanity, beauty and power. She bore no love for other human beings. Frightening and strange became her ways. Rigidity detested her new name intensely and tried to rigidly hold on to the previous one and to thus force the people to keep on calling her by it, but the people, like people like to do, persisted in calling Rigidity by the newest name they had given to her. And the harder she resisted it, the louder they called it.

It happened that, at this time, owing to her persistent attachment to old forms, her health broke down.

By the time she recovered, her face, older, less beautiful, remained marked by the deep scars of her illness and struggles, and there was a tired ring to her voice. And, for some unknown reason, the people at this point began to call her Lesson. They pointed at her and said: "Lesson, Lesson, Lesson!" And Lesson saw that they were but pointing her out to the new, young beauty in town and pointing out her own destiny to her too. Lesson was very dejected. Sadly she sneaked out of town in the dead of night and wandered lost and lonely, trying to put a finger on what exactly had gone wrong in her life. And Lesson spent many years trying to understand life. Many lonely years.

And during these years of her travels, fellow wayfarers who saw her simply dubbed her with the name Simplicity, for she walked silent and alone and appeared to do all her things simply. When Simplicity found out that this was her new name, it seemed to her that there was a hidden message and clue in this name. She then began to consciously strive to do all things simply, to think simply and to cultivate true simplicity of the soul. Finally Simplicity settled down in a little hut in a little village where she cultivated farms and gardens and grew to love children and nature.

The people of the village loved exceedingly this obviously aristocratic yet so modest, archaic stranger who had come to live amongst them and, inspired by her ways, they named her Humility. This name struck the surprised Humility with such great humbleness that she again, using it as a guiding star, started striving consciously after true humbleness and humility in her life, in order to become worthy of the name. Humility was ever ready to carry out even the lowliest of tasks and was never too proud to speak up for the truth when she saw it being denied, or even to fight for it, no matter how much of a fool she might appear in the eyes of others for doing so; for in her newfound humility it no longer mattered to her what others thought of her. Because true humility is strength, not weakness, as we all know.

The people of the village learnt much from Humility, who was by now rather an old woman, and gradually they recognised the absolute magnificence of the beautiful female spirit that occupied her old body – which revealed to them the essence of true inner beauty – and, unanimously, they agreed to change her name to Beauty! And so, for the second time in her life, Beauty was called Beauty again, but now for a genuine reason, for the truest of beauty is the beauty of the heart.

Many more years has Beauty now lived amongst the people of this dear and beautiful village, and it is Beauty herself who is now writing down her own long and eventful story. Except that now – now that this village has become a place of that true heavenlike peace and beauty which she has always borne hidden, deep, within her maturing soul – Beauty's name is no longer Beauty, but she now bears an other and final name which will be the one that will be etched unto her grave tablet when this old, warm body of hers is finally returned to earth. And what do you think this her ninth name is? – It might be Service; or Leadership; or Strength; it could be Love; or perhaps Peace; or even Heaven. It may also be Purity; or Guide; or Guardian; or maybe it could be Mirror. Choose for yourself, every woman out there, do.

I am simply what I should be.

Emptiness always makes the greatest noise. Would that emptiness could learn to become silent, that it may be true *and become filled*.

Goodbye, Earth.

The beautiful old woman died two days after writing down her own story; and when she was buried, the grateful village people inscribed upon her grave stone the single word... HOME.

Levels Of Understanding, Mountains Of Change, And No Horizons

...

THERE IS A land without a horizon. If you stand upon this land and stare with a keen gaze far into the distance, you will see, not a horizon, but at the farthest, most visible line, a mountain range.

And when you have arrived this Mountain range and climbed these difficult and painful Mountains of transformation you will, at their top, find yourself upon a plain, a plateau, which to your amazement you will realise to be the level surface of another land, another level, upon which you may stay and experience, or further wander. And when you again cast your gaze far into the distance, towards the East, there from where the light comes, you will one day see again, not a horizon, but another Mountain range...

And so we wandered, a band of insatiable restless seekers, from one level to the next, slowly coming to comprehend that life and development is an inner journey of many stages, arranging themselves like a flight of stairs in ascent, or descent, one step, one level, of maturity following upon the other. And as you climb the Mountain which is the end of one reality, so you ascend the Mountain which is the lowest point of another.

There came a day when we paused upon a plateau and, looking back, saw our past descending like a flight of giant steps behind us, curving gently downwards like a winding stairway round and round an invisible pillar of life, around which our gazes also bent. And as we followed the sight of the descending steps of our former levels, so did each of us recognise his and her own distinct footprint left upon each plain, silent, unobserved by those former friends and newly sighted wanderers we could see trudging down there upon those lands, standing around or shuffling left and right. For where we had seen Mountains and sought them, they had seen only a misty future and a horizon of clouds. And where we had felt restless, they had felt at home.

Like indelible lines on forgotten pages of an old book, our tracks marked the landscape of yesterday's land wherein our friends yet lived, waiting for changes they would have to bring about themselves. Then I understood why the old book keeps on changing from reader to reader, generation to generation and writer to writer – when you change the present, you change not just the future... you change also the past.

Like seeking thoughts groping their way through the lines of a sealed page, looking back I saw our former comrades wandering sightlessly round and round the footprints we left behind.

And then a few of them would notice the footprints, and maybe feel something happen inside their souls, and follow then them footprints with their eyes curiously... until, with a startled surprise, one or two would make out far in the distance, a mountain range where formerly they saw only a misty final horizon. Amazed they ask themselves where these mountains suddenly came from. Each mountain will be a hard climb, my friend, for with each upward step you must also actually climb over an obstacle which you bear within.

A word of hope for them. A word, a strong wish that flies back, like a bird, over to them; but not everyone will see the bird – only those looking up will. For these eastward-gazing people with a question gleaming deep in their eyes we whispered a word of hope..., and then we turned around again, to experience this new land upon which we stood.

Hard had been the ascent through the Mountains that led into this land, and one or two had fallen behind, trapped still in these mountains, unable yet to complete the transformation. But a few of us had indeed found the plateau at the top.

It was a strange land, for gaze as we may into the distance, on this one we saw no new mountains in the distant future... only land and clouds and a seeming horizon. It was a beautiful and mysterious land... and years have passed now since it has held us in its embrace. We have forgotten to look to the East, seeking the New... This new land has become, finally, our home. For many years now.

Some, I tell you, meanwhile have become bored here... and journeyed back down to their haunts of yore, welcomed back by many a comrade on a recycled rung, horizontal heroes of their own yesterdays. But the most have remained here on this new won plane, experiencing and experiencing...

Years of experiencing, experiences that satisfied some... but left a few seeking for something new. These few increasingly bear a thoughtful look upon their faces. Until one day they said to the rest of us, "Do you see these footsteps that disappear in that direction?" They pointed towards the clouds.

"No, we see them not," we replied, after following

their gaze.

"And do you see those Mountains far away in the distance?...

We raised our eyes and saw only clouds at the horizon.

"No, we see only clouds. There is nothing more, nowhere further. We have reached the summit."

But these Few would not be satisfied, and one day when we woke up, they were gone, restless souls, towards the cloudy mists in the future.

Often have I stood, silent, on my own, and gazed after their footsteps, for one of them, Kulie, had been my good friend. And I have gazed and gazed towards the Light coming through the clouds in the East. And sometimes when I intently gaze, my heart full of longing and a quietly persistent question, the clouds seem to disappear, and I slowly make them out, vaguely, rugged mountains of reflection, far far away. While on other days, when I simply curiously look across, all I see are clouds hovering above a final horizon. Quiet thoughts cross my mind.

I wonder if upon a mountain which I cannot yet see, a spirit pauses at this very moment, and turning around, sees me upon this level which he has left behind, sees the question in my eyes, and whispers for me a word of hope.

More and more, such questions arise within me. For as much as I love this strange and beautiful state of being, this mature level of thought, this comfort zone and stable throne, and my circle of friends who inhabit with me this point of view, yet stirs within me an old restlessness anew, urging me again to think ahead, to look up, for there is a new perception somewhere and no horizon comprehensible to me.

What are those mountains I increasingly seem to see there, in the distance? Inviting and imposing at the same time. Peaceful and rugged. Why should I brave them if indeed they do exist? But, if they do, what land lies again upon them? Maybe somebody stands upon them now and whispers words of hope for me. And maybe these thoughts I think, and think are mine, in truth are his, calling me, talking to me -

"Seeking spirit, be sure of one thing: there is always something more..."

Mountains and Valleys

...

WHEN YOU REACH the mountainpeak, you cannot take off like a bird, you cannot fly up and away like a bird, because you are not a bird, nor do you have the wings of a bird. Nay, you are human.

But in you is a bird. It is your volition, your prayer, the voice of your spirit. So, set it free upon your mountainhigh, whence you can no longer upwards step. Set your bird free in your stead and it will take up to heaven that part of you which has asked for it, and there it shall add another thread, another colour, another design into the weaving of the heavenly gown that awaits you Tomorrow.

Then keep moving, you, move on, down the incline ahead of you, into the next valley of abiding and human experiencing and deep inner maturing.

And as you crown them one by one, the mountain-peaks of your distant self, as you release bird after bird from your maturing heart, slowly you overcome the world, slowly you mount the one great spiritual mountain, until you arrive at its peak; and, this time, it is your voice that will return downwards into the valley, to encourage and guide your fellow wanderers, whilst you, the spirit, will shed your cloak and float upwards into the bright morning kingdom of spirit and activity in the light of the rays of a thousand suns.

And upon you and your Home and the lights of your home shall beam down the Radiance of the inexhaustible, faithful Love of God, pulsating downwards from the Fountainhead of the Grail.

The Wheel of Fortune

...

TWO MEN in search of fortune.

Said the first:
"I will stay and farm my father's land!"

Said the second:
"I will go and find the Wheel of Fortune, and I will turn it in my direction, and I shall possess it and I shall wield it, and I shall be a controller of happenings, a decider of destinies."

Said the first:
"You will come back and beg me for a little plot of land on which to farm."

Said the second:
"You will seek me and plead with me to turn your fortunes around with the Wheel of Fortune."

Said the first:
"You cannot find the Wheel of Fortune. It is not a physical thing that can be grasped with the hand or seen with the eye. It is a power which started as a concept. It is everywhere."

Said the second:
"It is a power which started as a concept and ended up as a wheel, a physical wheel that can be grasped with the hand and seen with the eye. I will find it and I will place a firm hold on it. It shall be mine. The Wheel of Fortune. Fortune!"

Said the Spirit of Fortune:
"The sooner you start, the better."

The years have gone by and still he seeks. Through fortune and misfortune, through pleasure and pain, he seeks the wheel of fortune, that he may become a controller of happenings, a decider of destinies.

Said the first:
"The years have passed. Fortune, which smiled at me

in the first few years, frowns now upon me. The harvest is meager. The earth sits hard upon me. Where is my friend who went to seek the Wheel of Fortune? I must find him. He will surely turn the wheel in my favour, and the winds shall turn in kind."

Said the second:
"The years have passed. My wandering feet thirst for rest, my restless heart for peace. I have searched everywhere, in vain. I must return to my friend. Surely he will find for me a little plot of land where I can seek my fortune and fulfill my destiny."

Said the Spirit of Fortune:
"The sooner you go, the better."

Said the Spirit of Fortune:
"The sooner you return, the better."

They met again upon the Highway at the halfway point between the going and the returning.

Said the first:
"My friend, have you found the Wheel of Fortune now? For you must turn it my way. The soil is unyielding, the farm is fruitless."

Said the second:

"No, I have not found the wheel of fortune and was just on my way to you, that you may find me a little of your land where I may seek my fortune, for the road grows weary beneath my feet."

Said the first:
"But you assured me that the Wheel of Fortune is a findable physical thing."

Said the second:
"And you assured me that the land would one day support both of us!"

Said the first:
"The land is a deceiver, now I know. It is the whore of fortune and only does his bidding. I shall go now and find the Wheel of Fortune. Then shall I own the land."

Said the second:
"Oh, my friend, but you err. Fortune has no wheel. Myths have given birth to this belief. The land is the key to fortune. The land is the wheel of fortune. Possess the land and you have grasped fortune's wheel."

Said the first:
"I have turned the land several times, sometimes with my pitchfork, other times with a multitude of other implements such as my shovel, my hoe and my fin-

gers, but not once did my fortune lastingly turn, although I turned the earth repeatedly. Sometimes the winds turned, briefly, but fortune never really. Thus I act with full clarity today. You can have the land if you wish. I shall find the Wheel of Fortune and I shall possess it and I shall wield it and I shall be a controller of happenings, a decider of destinies."

Said the second:
"When you return to me, begging me to return your father's land to you, I shall not do so. For it is now mine! Bear this in mind."

Said the first:
"When you come to me, pleading with me to turn the Wheel of Fortune in your favour, I shall not do so! I shall abandon you to your fate. Bear this in mind."

Said the second:
"Oh, you fool, why will you not come that we may together plough the land?! Two pairs of hands will soften its heart. There is no physical Wheel of Fortune! It is a power that began as a concept."

Said the first:
"Fortune is a person. He bears a face and owns a wheel. I shall find him and I shall take the wheel from him. Then shall I turn the wheel against him. My wheel."

Said the Spirit of Fortune:
"The earlier you proceed, the better."

The years passed by like the wind, and old age crept upon them. The land softened and yielded rich harvests, but Fortune and his wheel refused to be found.

Said the first:
"I am old and grey. My days are numbered, my memories rich and poor. I shall return to my father's land and there shall I lay down, for I do not want to die upon the road."

Said the second:
I am old and grey. My days are numbered, my memories many and few. I shall set off again after the Wheel of Fortune, that I may turn it and prolong my life and reactivate the youth in me. If I die now, all is lost and I shall be buried upon another man's land. But if Fortune, who has smiled at me through the land, permits me now to find his wheel, then I shall change the course of my future."

Said the Spirit Fortune:
"Hurry, hurry, time is."

Said the Spirit of Fortune:

"Hurry, hurry, time is."

Their paths crossed again, this time at the junction that leads everybody on.

Said the first:
"Why are you here? Have you not mastered the land which for you is the wheel of fortune?"

Said the second:
"I am tired of you. Please, move out of my way. Your father's land is there. You can have it if you wish. Die on it; you are old enough for that now. I will have nothing to do with it anymore. It has brought me nothing but comfort, and prevented me from seeking the Wheel of Fortune, which was the ardent spiritual goal of youth! Look at me: now I am an old man."

Said the first:
"Then you shall die upon the road. I hope somebody finds you and buries you. I shall conclude my earthly wanderings there where I belong."

Said the second:
"Rest in peace. Adieu."

And then they parted ways, never to meet again upon the earth.

Said Fortune:
"Another twist, another turn,
And life goes on...
If they ask, or seek, or yearn
All I can do is turn and point them on...
The path they must go themselves -
The change they must work themselves
The moment they must grasp themselves -
The seeds of fortune they must sow themselves -
I am just a referee...

"Though men pass me by a thousand times
Never do they recognise me;
Nor is it necessary, as long as they heed
The Inner Voice in them that speaks to me.

"For I must obey, I must obey...
And place what they ask for upon their way."

Friends Forever

...

SOI AND TEMI were friends right from the very beginning, friends forever, friends for life.

They explored the ancient forbidden caves together which none may enter who wish to remain unchanged. But whoever enters and emerges alive will never ever be the same again.

The thirst for adventure, the hunger for something new, bid them enter these caves, and together they did, like they had, united, entered every adventure before, brother with brother, friend for friend.

No-one ever came to know what they experienced within the caves, no-one, but indeed when they emerged a wondrous change had been wrought upon Soi and Temi. For upon the face of the quiet, philosophic Soi where peace and calm had been wont to rest, there now raged flashing thunder and restlessness beyond compare! But whereas Temi had entered the caves impetuous, carefree and wild, a rested sage with weathered eyes came walking out instead.

It did not take them both long to understand that they no longer got on with each other like they had once done. And all who met them now, who once had known them before they visited the ancient, forbidden caves, could not but marvel at this uncanny development: For save for their faces and save for their names, Soi had become Temi and Temi had turned to Soi. Indeed they might as well have switched identities.

But – and here's the wonder – whereas quiet Soi had interwoven well with carefree Temi, the new Soi, the restless, was a stranger to the new Temi, the silent, and *vice* versa.

The mystery of opposites, parallels and poles began to dawn on the people; for characters which had once so perfectly blended were now as distant as the poles. And clucking and clacking and clicking-a-clack the elders and superstitioners verily nodded and wisely declared that the knowledge of the ancients can never but never ever prove wrong: None may enter the ancient forbidden caves who wants to re-emerge the same!

But neither Soi nor Temi heard them speak, for

they were already a-separated and a-gone, the formerly peace-loving Soi to now be a warrior fighting on distant battlefields in the cause of unknown folk; the one-time aggressive Temi to traverse faraway lands, teaching strangers how to love and about peace.

Moments, as they are wont to do, passed by quick in time, hurrying through the modules of mortality; and before the stars had fully registered the change, the warrior Soi, at the head of a battalion of fiery foreign legions, came a-thundering into a land which for long had provoked their warring skills.

Burning and a-looting and a-screaming and a-hacking, they emerged victorious one phase after the other of battle, until they entered the capital where a mysterious sage preached calm and love and gently enjoined peace on all, attackers and defenders alike.

A brief din in the battle... Soi and Temi stood one before the other and neither recognised his brother, for if times change a man, his profession will change him even more.

The softly spoken words of the strange, gentle preacher finely pricked the conscience of the fiery, impatient warrior, for he too well remembered once long ago when he had known them true. But rather than yield to their truth and risk appearing a fool – which he never would have appeared, for it is the fool who resists truth and the great man who bows down

– he drew his sword and struck at this disturbing preacher with very mortal mien!

But, lo and behold, the preacher was neither surprised nor unprepared for the attack, for he too could well remember how hard it is for an unrestrained heart to accept that it is wrong, since he himself once upon a time one such brash heart had been. But neither too had he forgotten the ways to fend off a blow, for once a fighter, always a fighter indeed.

He dodged the lethal blow and fled. But the inflamed warrior pursued hard, accompanied by seven of his soldiers.

Hills, plains, woods were met and left behind as the warrior and his horde slowly closed the gap between them and the preacher. Finally, mounting a plateau, they surrounded the fleeing preacher.

However, among the warrior's seven soldiers, there was one whose heart had been secretly but deeply touched by the words of the preacher. And as he saw the preacher about to be knifed down by their daggers, he suddenly turned on his own men and slew two with a double-dealt blow. In the confusion that ensued, the preacher, seeing his chance, picked up a fallen dagger and turned on the warrior.

Their fight was brief for, wonders oh, the preacher was a warrior too and an even abler one than his once dear friend, the one time philosopher; and now that his death seemed a-near he'd quickly shed his gentle ways and a reckless fighter lay unveiled!

It was only as the warrior crashed down and lay upon the ground, dying, dagger incisions in him, his red blood a-pooling, that the senselessness of his legacy and the futility of his quest, thus ending, arrested and animated his insight. His original self, as from a deep slumber, re-awakened – and he spoke… spoke on futility, stupidity, humanity. The battle ceased and in wonder all parties gazed at the expiring warrior for, in his hour of death, he had re-turned into a philosopher, gentle, wise and convincing.

With dimming eyes he gazed up at the eyes and into the soul of his shocked and startled killer and, in a clear flash, suddenly recognised in this reckless fighter-of-a-priest but his own old gregarious friend, Temi.

"Oh Temi, my friend, oh Temi, my friend." he whispered with a tender smile, "What Nemesis is it that has decreed that I die in your hands…?"

With hands still a-poised for the final blow, for indeed his old self had true awakened, Temi paused…

A thunderbolt come down from the skies would surely not have shocked him as still as Soi's still whisper did…

"Soi?" he whispered.

"Temi…" came Soi's replied.

And then he died.

The Man-Child

...

ONCE, AS I stood outside my house early one dawn, I saw the man-child playing in front of my door.
I called to him:

Child of Creation! What brings you here?
He turned around, looked into my eyes with his bright, warming eyes.

I came to visit the world, he said, *to learn its ways and woes.*

I left my family and people, and went to the man-child, vowing to protect him from evil men. He, however, did not understand my vow, for he was yet to understand evil men.

And so we set off together, to learn him the world.
We first came across the weary and the poor, and

the man-child smiled at them; and his smile, like the sun, melted their sorrows away. He told them stories of life in the higher realms of creation; and his stories, like gentle rain and cool breezes, calmed them and made them sleep, peacefully.

As we journeyed on, the man-child grew into an adolescent. Then we came across the entertainers and singers. He joined them and began to sing with them. That was the first time I noticed that little thing which would one day lead to much sorrow. It was obvious that the man-child was a better entertainer, and soon the others became jealous. But because he was still something of a boy, it would have seemed very foolish if they had expressed these feelings openly. So instead they said that he was an adolescent and should not be with men. They drove him away. As he walked away, I saw confusion mixed with sadness in his eyes, and I did my best to distract him from his inner pain.

Meanwhile the man-child grew into a youth and we came across the workers and the farmers. The youth asked for a chance to work, got it. But his work was the most beautiful and soon he became the recipient of the majority of the customers. The fruit of his farm was also the richest, and in no time more and more of the market-visitors came buying from him. The other workers and farmers grew angry, envious. And they planned against him; and, going to the scholars and the lawmakers, they bore false witness against him.

So the scholars and lawmakers summoned him and he explained his soul, whereupon it became apparent that he was innocent and it was the others who had lied. He became a hero.

By now he had grown into a man, and the scholars and lawmakers bid him stay with them for they perceived a keen intelligence behind his luminous eyes.

He consented, and stayed. But in no time at all, it became clear that the scholars were ignorant and the lawmakers themselves lawbreakers, because the man-child's wisdom was like a bright light that illumined all inherent defects, much to the displeasure of the scholars and lawmakers. If it became apparent to all that he was wiser than they, that would be the end of their position of prominence and their status. So they promulgated a law deliberately designed to ensnare him, through which they arrested him for being a stranger and a deceiver.

But before they could sentence him to his punishment, I ran ahead to the elders and the custodians of truth, before whom I laid down the entire matter.

All parties were summoned.

I remember that day clearly. Everybody was sitted except the man-child. He stood in their middle and he was no more a child, but a man. His lips were formed into a perpetual, if subtle, half-smile, interrupted by lines of sorrow and a slight furrow on his forehead that both told more than the bitterest words would. Tears ran down my cheeks as I saw what the world had done to the beautiful, innocent child of creation. Presiding over the sitting was the Prince of the Land, their highest authority. He too summoned himself to the sitting, for no case in recent history had been imbued with so much intrigue or attracted so much publicity.

And voices began to speak. To accuse. But when the man in the heart of the child of creation spoke, it became clear that the lawmakers were the lawbreakers and the scholars ignorant.

The Prince, he was a good man, he decided to let the man-child go free. But the elders were afraid and the custodians of truth were no real custodians of truth, for they realised that if the man in the heart of the child of creation continued speaking, he would soon show that even they were less than they were supposed to be.

They informed the Prince that if he did not convict the stranger, then he would gather enormous power, wealth and force-of-arm, and overthrow the Prince. When the Prince heard this, his fear and ego flared up within him. He charged the man-child to speak again and to make clear his position with regards to this accusation.

The man-child, however, having understood what was going on, shook his head and remained silent. His lips were turned down. No smile played on them any longer.

The Prince became confused. Finally he let the executioners execute the murdering of the man-child, lest he indeed become greater then he was and overthrow him.

It was a bright, hot noon, the day on which he was executed for being the child of creation. Nature wept. Hours later, I walked away, remembering the times we had shared. Remembering his sunny heart. My heart broke. Then broke doubly. For I saw that the people were celebrating the murder of the troublesome stranger.

As my weeping grew deeper, a Shadow fell upon me. I looked up and saw the Avenger looking down on us all. And he was not smiling.

A Headlong Fall

...

SHE WAS LONGING for the deep. A headlong fall into the dark abyss. There was something at the bottom, the sightless depths, that pulled her with irresistible power, like a magnet. She stood perched on the edge of the precipice and stared longingly, anxiously, searchingly into the waiting bowels of the darkness and felt the pull, the call. If a hand had reached out from the deep, a giant hand, she would have clutched on to it with hers and gone down with it, down to the source of the great pull.

But she could not. The precipice in its precarious noncrossability, the abyss in its treacherously easy availability, were also a wall. A non-permeable wall that divided her from her longing, bound her to her state.

There was a sunlit meadow behind her and to her ears arrived the twittering of a hundred birds. That was her life. The life of which she had tired. Yet the strings of that life bound her fast. She could not go beyond the boundary of the precipice. The call of the deep would remain unanswered. Her longing would stay unfulfilled. But how could she bear it? How could she go on like this day after day with this pull in her soul without being able to resolve it?

She longed for the deep.

The deep was mirrored in his eyes. His look was the reflection of the deep that was sunk into his soul. In him were the deep and the call of the mysterious magnet down at the sightless bottom of the deep. It was in his voice, in the turn of his head, in his hands and the way they first held her. It was in his slow measured walk and accurate mental deliberations. It was on his lips, it was the low-cut hair on his head, it was around him, within him. It was he.

He drew her with such an intensity, such a passion, that she was perpetually on the verge of crying out, loud, sharp, desperate, wired out of control... yet she did not. Because, most of all, he made her *calm*.

She first met him one day at the beach. It was a public holiday. May 29th, 2000. Democracy Day in Nigeria. It was the first time this day was being celebrated, amidst controversy of course. The labour union bore down heavily on the president for having unilaterally declared, of all days, May 29th henceforth as Democracy Day, a public holiday. The Upper and Lower Houses had a field day president-bashing. But in the end the day stayed.

Uninterested in political matters, she had gone to the beach on this day with her friend, Hadiza, happy to spend time with the roaring, in the sight and nearness, of the ocean. Born and bred in Lagos, the sea had all her life been her secret lover.

The beach was full. She liked the noise that pressed in on the great hall of silence in her centre. The contrast gave her a kick. Here deep within her the silence. Outside, beyond the silence and hall of silence, the noise, not only of the crowded beach, the overcrowded world, but also of her thoughts which had to think extra loud – or was it *extra quietly* – extra clearly today in order for her to hear them.

And everything was centred on the waves. They crashed, cracked and thundered... yet the sea of silence remain unruffled, for in the heart of the roaring waves too was the silence.

The silence of the eternal sea of life. Deep space bordered by horizon.

She stood on the sand dune and looked beyond the rising shoulders of the waves and out into the Atlantic. Creamy pale blue and watching you.

What was in there? And beyond it, *what?*

Stirred by this question, her soul was, like a sensitive gland, activated, perceptive, ready.

Before she saw him, she *sensed* him. The deep was coming closer. The deep!

At first she thought it must be the ocean.

That far place. Horizon.

She looked at it... longingly. But her longing met no response from there. It was not the ocean. It was... it was...

Her heart leaped and she looked around wildly. Never before had the deep exercised such a physical presence. So she was prepared for him when their eyes met. The longing and the yearning. By and by.

A shock wave arose from the deep, the earth at the precipice trembled.

Later he found an excuse to saunter up to them.

He spoke about the beach, the water, the public holiday. He spoke intelligently. He spoke to her. His name was Anosike, he worked in an oil company, he said, played the guitar in his spare time. She got up and they went on a stroll. Patiently they sought out the quietest, most secluded area of the rainforest beach. She put her hand in his. It was large and enclosed hers completely. The sun was high and bright beyond the fronds. Then. Everything has a boundary, if not an end. It was clear right from the very first that he had come to get her. She did not think of resisting.

Unhesitatingly, unafraid, she stepped forward and fell into the deep.

And all the while, his voice. It was an unending process.

The ties that had hitherto pulled her back, they were no more. Nothing stopped her. Nothing inhibited her.

Only once, for a wisp of a microsecond, did she remember the sunlit meadow. Then the momentum tilted her gently forward and, headlong, the blood rushed up and she fell...

A desperate cry floated up... and that was the last that was heard of her.

Touching A Flower

...

THERE ARE FRIENDS you know that you have stored deep within your heart. These friends are blown in by the wind, borne in by a river... a golden river. There are people you know that even if you were parted from them, you would never forget them... There are spirits which share with you a part of your wanderings through creation. Those to whom you entrust your secrets, knowledge about your faults and questions and contradictions... and you know that you are one. That you share so many similar things.

A flower. Who can touch, who can break, who can soil a flower? Who dares? A speaking bird once said to me: "Life is a forest, a jungle, full of wild trees, wild fruits and wild beasts, wild sounds and hunters and preys and the sounds of the forest. You will meet everything, each thing in its own place. Separated according to their species. But there is one thing which you will see everywhere. Always you will see a flower somewhere.

"It will appear unexpectedly from beneath hidden rocks, betwixt twisted trunks, hover above unreachable branches, glow in the rays of the moon, there will always be a flower somewhere.

"Think not that every flower you meet you are permitted to touch...

"Though they warm your heart, raise your spirits, brighten your soul, relieve your mind, inspire you and encourage you..., yet think twice before you touch a flower, consider well before you pick one off its stem. Maybe the simple pleasure that the sight of it has given you, is all it is supposed to bring you. Ask yourself: are you worth it? Will it blossom and bloom in your hands as beautifully as it blossoms and blooms on its own? Is the soil of your heart ready to keep a flower alive? If not, wait... wait for when you will be ready to touch it and plant it in your heart. There will always be one flower waiting for you...

"And should you wander into the desert of life too, your longing to see a flower is what shall see you through. Yet shall your longing not be in vain. For you bear your flower within. Always within. Watered by your love, sunned by your gratitude, rooted in your heart, it will always bloom by your side."

And so I set forth... but I confess that her words I forgot. Many a flower that delighted my heart I snapped and inhaled and left to wither by the roadside. So crashed I triumphantly through the jungle like a King, littering the path behind me with the fading sadness of flowers I had touched and crushed and left to wither in my restless memory.

In the desert it is eerie and burns like a furnace. Thorns bleed my bare feet, one for every flower I once carelessly crushed. How I long now for a flower, for the sight of a flower again. This eternal desert which the forest has become. I remember all the flowers that litter my past. Would that I had planted just one inside my heart, in my life.

Yet there is one. Brief had been our meeting, short my sight of her. I had reached for her, but strong branches had kept her beyond my reach. The speaking bird had hovered on the branches around her, singing into her ears. Her smile was all I got, and oh how this I treasured. She alone comes back to my mind now, over and over and over again. And as I trudge on through the desert, following the bird that appears and disappears, it is the hope of seeing her again that keeps me alive.

The one flower I left unhurt is the one that shall heal my wound.

The Two Songs

...

ONCE UPON A time, two birds became friends in a faraway country, different from their own. They decided to make two songs, not just one...

Then they said goodbye and each bird returned to a different country.

Music is a country. Loneliness is a country. But love would like to visit all countries and free all peoples.

I still know our two songs and, tomorrow, when all countries have united in love to be one world, I'll teach you another song you once wanted to sing...

Do not be afraid to open up your heart because there are two songs in there, not one.

Two Of Them Seekers

...

BUT WHAT WOULD it be like now, if right now you suddenly stood before me again in all your beauty?

I know what it would be like, yes I do. It would be like the first outcry of joy that arose in the moment of creation. It would be like the first indescribable knowing of joy when the first prayer was answered. Nay, when the first prayer was uttered.

Imagine what it is. You do not know God, nor that He exists. And then, in a moment of danger, suddenly you pray – and, remember, you never knew anything about prayer – but, in that moment of danger, you pray: *Help!*

You feel the prayer rip its way out of you and you feel your plea rise up in the column of prayer, and connect something somewhere far away, from where the answer flows into you. You feel it flow in. Your perception changes. – And you want to know what just happened – thus do you begin to seek.

In your seeking, you stumbled upon me, another seeker, we journeyed a while together, then parted ways.

Please, when you find more answers, remember me and let them flow to me too, to me too, and the same I promise you too, tonight. –

Waiting

...

THERE IS a man in the Nsukka hills. If you drive past between 7 and 8 pm in the evening and look up with sharpened eyes, you might see his outline. Some say he is mad. Others say he is not. But all know and say that he is waiting...

He is waiting for his love, his heart, who promised to meet him there – *thirty-two years ago!*

They met by chance and fell in love also by chance. Then came a terrible civil war in the land which forced them to part from each other and disappear in different directions for different reasons. But before they parted they promised to meet one another again on these hills as soon as the war was over.

They stood upon these hills and made the promise.

Then they departed.

The war, as all wars do, eventually ended... a full thirty-two years ago. He came to the agreed hills and began to wait. But she did not appear.

He must be sixty now, or fifty, or seventy; it's hard to tell. He looks ageless. Only his eyes betray an age indefinable with words which, if one were to attempt to but articulate, can only be captured with the expression *ever-young*.

He believes she will come. He believes that she loved and still loves him just as strongly as he loved and still loves her; and any love that strong does not break its own vows; for if they can be broken, they would not have been spoken.

But people have sworn that she died in the war.

Others declare that they have seen her in a distant land in the west, married and happy.

And yet not a few maintain mournfully that she did indeed come back once, took a look at him from afar, then turned around and walked away again.

Anytime he hears any of these stories, he does not get angry, neither does he laugh. He does not dismiss them offhandedly or obstinately, no. Instead he raises his eyes, sea-deep and dead-serious, to the heavens and keeps them there for a long, long time. Then, finally, slowly, a warm smile would begin to glow on his face as he brought his bright eyes back to bear upon the speaker or speakers, informing them in a voice as unperturbed as the pacific:

"No... she is on the way..."

Those who have met him say he is a nice friendly fellow, jovial and communicative... half-the-time. The other half he is silent and lonely, wondering what could be taking her *so long*. In such moments, he is sorrowful, thoughtful.

I mounted the hill at the appropriate evening hour to find, see and meet this wonder for myself. My heart pounded. He is truly a legend, a hero, made of that fractionless primevium of which immortals are forged. Thirty-two years and he is still waiting, waiting, waiting for a dream... - can I do that too?

The rising moon was fuller. What would he have to say to me?

I saw his silhouette, like a human mountain, noble and undefeated, backing me, face raised to the moon, breathing, still. I approached as silently as I could, so as not to disturb the solemnity of this magic moment.

As I neared him, I saw him raise his two hands skywards for one steady arrested moment in time, like a victor, his body shuddered; then he turned around and faced me, tears and laughter in his eyes.

"Darling, what took you so long?" he whispered at me...

I had been sure that I would not cry, but now the last chains broke and fell from my heart and I ran to him, fell into his embrace, weeping uncontrollably.

Indeed what had taken me so long? I do not know. Why do we lose courage in the greater and settle for the lesser? Why do we always fear the immortal call of love? Why did I hesitate for *thirty-two long years* to do the one single thing that I have longed more than every other thing in the world to do? And to thereby fulfil my eternal promise. What had so scared me? The notion of eternal love or the possibility of betrayal?

And all the while he had waited, waited for me, surer than I was that I would return to my destiny...

Love cannot die.

The Villager

...

ONCE UPON A time, in a village near Enugu, nestling in the luscious green valleys between the plateaus of the Udi hills, in south-eastern Nigeria, there settled a city-dweller, a young urbanite, come to hide from fellow city dwellers and indeed the city itself in the quiet of this peaceful village.

At first the quiet laze of the unhurried village folk was a great delight to him and a welcome change from the impersonal razzmatazz of the city. However, after some time there arose in him an itch, product of a silent but powerful addiction to city-life which, unknown to him, had become a part of his constitution.

The restless itch became exacerbated to the point where he was about to abandon all hope of a more fulfilling existence in the rural and resort back to the urban.

That was when he met the villager.

Previously he had only seen him fleetingly, as he went to or returned from his farm, presunrise and postsunset, without ever clearly discerning his features or exchanging a word or direct gaze with him.

But did dusk descend later than usual upon this fateful day? Or did the villager's own restlessness propel him out of his farm, setting him homebound, earlier than usual?

It could be anything.

But as the city-dweller looked up from his front door, there he saw the familiar fleeting figure... only this time he was much more visible in the hanging lights of mesmerizingly tantalisingly unhurried sunset.

For the first time he saw the villager's features and, lo and behold, he was a young man just like himself; but his face appeared to have been chiselled out of smooth, hard stone, fired in flames like metal ore, and then brought to life by a soft breath from heaven. For the eyes which momentarily seized the city-dweller's, though set in the most rugged of features, were gentle and kind. Suddenly they seemed so similar, these two very unsimilar men.

Only for a moment did these two men lock gaze and then the villager looked again ahead of him and, sack in hand, hoe slung over his shoulder, sturdily yet gracefully walked on home, a half-spring, half-unspring, in his heels, a man freely born to farm his village land, oblivious to everything else, happy and content in his destiny.

The next day the city-dweller packed his belongings and returned to his home in the city. He had found what he came to the village searching for. He had found and become the villager in his heart.

Foreverevermore

...

ONCE UPON a time in south-southern Nigeria, high up on the misty Obudu plateaux of those dreamy Sankwala mountain-ranges of which we only hear and read, but hardly ever see, there lived a voiceless girl called Iwi.

Iwi loved the air of the mountain-peak, she loved the clouds which sometimes came visiting, she loved the heavened birds that loved these same heights which she also loved; she loved the stars that shone brightly in the evenings, mornings and through the nights.

Iwi, being a little maiden, did not live alone. She lived with her mother, whom she called "Sister", and who called her "Iwi, my friend", for theirs was a deep and true friendship. Iwi's father had also once lived with them and in those days they had been a happy triangle. In those days her voice had still been with her, and her childlike songs and happy chatter had delighted her parent's heart. Until one day her father died mysteriously, leaving Iwi and her mother to be each all the other had. The day her father died was the day Iwi lost her voice. As though he had taken it with her, try as she might, no sound ever again escaped her lips.

Iwi and her mother could have gone to live in any of the cities in the valleys where life would have been easier for them, but they loved these mountain-highs and preferred to live in hardship but preserve peace of soul. So up in the mountains they stayed, where they sensed their heart to be, and happiness kept them company every day. Together they reared the goats, tended the fowl, cultivated the farms and the gardens of those rare fruits that grew on those high climates, and rarely, but rarely, did they go down all the way to the valley, mainly to the Sankwala market, indeed just when they had to go.

As mysteriously as Iwi's father had left the earth, her mother died one day, leaving Iwi now all alone upon their mountain home. If her father's departure had taken her voice away, her mother's did not bring it back, voiceless she remained.

After burying her mother, Iwii made the decision

to continue to live up there where mountain-air, mountain-clouds and mountain-sighs gave back to her the love she gave. But lonely was she now, alone in the world, if we forget the the goats, the fowl and the flowers, and of course the fairies she saw not, although they saw her, and the friendy stars in the skies - all of which we may however not forget. Yet none of them proved able to restore to her her once beautiful voice.

She grew into a woman and grew used to being a single woman on the heights, managing and flowing, but once in a while longing for another human.

One day, like a miracle, who did she see walking there upon her mountains? A hermit, but younger than most hermits are, more handsome than hermits ought to be. If she was full surprised, then surely she was not half as surprised as he was... to find this beautiful woman living, alone, high up there where he'd come seeking solitude, hoping to discover himself in silence. So, shyly, he avoided her for the next couple of months and shyly she pretended too that he was not up there.

But then one morning, like a man must do, he waited for her outside her mountain hut. And when she emerged he, in the Obanliku dialect of these parts, introduced himself to her and offered her a small basket of wild *ụdara* which he had gathered early that morning as the sun's rays were still struggling to break through the mountain mist.

It is hard to say how long she stood there, silent, surprised, staring at him; but however long it was must have been of no consequence, for just as long did he too remain standing there, refusing to budge, waiting for her to reply. The moment was broken when, to her utmost shock, she heard her voice thanking him and then telling him her name. They both smiled as she accepted the basket of wild berries from him and then he turned around and walked away.

And so did they gradually they began to stop, to talk, one word here, two words there. And finally, over a year after he first arrived these heights, they began to live together. That he was a stranger to these parts was clear to her, for she heard it in his accent, although he bravely struggled to speak her thongue. It did not matter to her, it only made her love him all the more.

Love and understanding and joy are three things which when they arrive at the same time, in the same place, around the same people, create that thing which words cannot describe. And so it was between Iwi and the young hermit whose name, as he had told her that fateful morning, was Sike. Their love was eternal, immortal, intense - and it never ceased to startle them.

Through Iwi, Sike came to see and understand the

Obudu mountains and their lush green forests with new eyes; its moods became a dictionary of new language upon his heart; mist or rain, animals or fauna, plauteaux or gorges, forests and waterfalls, his senses became born again to a world that was part of his native country but which he had never known, for it was so different from the world he came from that he knew he would never be able to describe it to the people of his world, villagers and city-people alike. And the more he discovered nature, the more he loved this beautiful female spirit who was the source of his rebirth. Everything that was special about this place was reflected in her nature - everything that was special about her personality was reflected in this cradle of nature. How could the one be separated from the other? The source of his joy became the emblem of his sorrow.

For just when Iwi came to believe that Sike would stay up here with her, forevermore. he told the truth about himself: he was a servant of his people who had come here to seek quietude and clarity, but had vowed to return to his people when he was done, to continue with his service. He spoke about communal clashes and border disputes, about social projects and missions of hope and other things he was not sure she understood. Without emotion Iwi listened to him and then, with trembling heart, waited for him to ask her if she would come with him, not knowing what her answer would be.

But the request never came. She did not ask him if there was someone else waiting for him in his old life, nor did he mention it.

Now Sike stood outside Iwi's hut, looked at the sky, and tear on tear fell from his eyes. He'd come up here to find understandings rare, only to end up with much more than he had expected. After strengthening his heart with a silent prayer which Iwi did not see, but strongly felt, he turned to her and said:

"Iwi... I love you... eternally... but I love also the people I have pledged to serve, and I love the service I have vowed to fulfill all the days of life... they need me... and so I must return there where I came from."

They held each other tightly one last time under the blue skies, tropical avians winging their way over, and he promised to love her... and she promised to love him... foreverevermore...

They parted on that same evening - Iwi remained with his heart upon her Obudu mounain-tops, Sike took her heart with him to his calling.

She never did find out to which constituency he belonged, he never came to know what became of her in the future; but every morning and every evening, both their heartborn, love-borne thoughts meet in the firmaments of Heaven, and their thoughts promise love foreverevermore.

iii.

When I look
within

...

A Poet's Heart

...

SOMETIMES THE night is so incredibly beautiful, I wish it would last a little longer tonight. Everywhere, everything is so soft. The night air is cool, soft. The vibration of the world, of my neighbourhood, has lost its harshness and it seems as though everybody loves everybody tonight. And I am glad again that I was born a poet.

I will live a poet and when I die, the world will say: a poet is gone. And if the world mourns, then I will be glad I disappointed the world and became a poet instead of a lawyer, engineer, banker, doctor, scientist, professor emeritus.

The poem that I wanted to write on the day I took the decision and forsook the world, I have now forgotten. Forgotten if I even wrote it at all or whether I kept it back in, bolted up in the hall of silence in my soul, where I continued to nourish it, and perhaps only wrote it another day in another poem, or maybe I've not even written it yet.

And yet, for its sake, and for the sake of a thousand and more poems yet unwritten, I disobeyed, ignored and disappointed the world, I dropped out of school, forsook a supposedly great destiny and became just a poet struggling to get by.

And yet I know, when I die they will say wistfully, with wet eyes: *a poet is gone...*

And they will feel it in their hearts. –

So poets are special afterall.

Sometimes the night is so beautiful and I wish it would last a little longer tonight, and I'm glad I was born a poet. Even when I'm dead and gone I'll leave behind upon the sad earth a few lines that will forever move human hearts and they will nod thoughtfully and say: *once upon a time, a poet was born... he lived on earth, he wrote poems and he died...*

They will say this because poems don't die and, in truth, poets too are immortal. None is so immortal as they that cook with letters, build with words and touch us not with fingers or lips, pictures or songs, as precious as these are, for who can live without love and kindness, music and art, but there is a special quality of perception that works wonders and magic within us when *language*, this device we so casually misuse and abuse everyday, is made into the container and preserver for generations to come of something that goes right into our core and makes us glad that the poet did not fail to write once upon a time.

And last night it was so beautiful. I was all alone and only once was I called upon, in the night, by the rain... it was at my window, poetic, heavenly, cold, sweet and temporary... it passed away, and took with it the last traces of the receding harmattan.

And I hoped the night would for once last a little longer last night, yet knew my hope was folly. Twice I slept anew, twice awoke, and the night was still with us and still so soft, and I thought of you, in the night.

And I slept again and when I opened my eyes the sun was shinning, the night is gone and I began to write this story of all that happens and happens never, but remembered ever by the works of the poetic spirit.

Birds are chirping. People are yapping outside my window too. Lagos is beautiful only at night when Nepa provides us with electricity and the fan or A/C is working, or else it needs must rain and the roof better not be leaking. But if you are lucky, you have a generator. Or a guitar. Best of all of course is the cooling cooling rain.

That is when Lagos is most beautiful. When the
Water falls...

I thirst after you
            Waterfall
I want to
Drink you up

        I am
The quivering starving lake
Underneath the Souls of
Your feet

Step on me
I will carry you to your river
            I am your horizon
You are my ocean.

The reading is taking place next Saturday. Who will
be there? Nobody I know, naturally. Of course they
will all think I know them and they know me. We will
shake hands and call one another by our names and
remember some incidents from the populous empty
past.

Yet I know them not and they know me not. We
are all strangers to one another. This is the city, where
neighbours and friends and strangers are all strangers to one another, and the city is the strangest one

of all amongst us, the laughing, mute, cunning, open, mocking, sorrowing city. Community of strangers and, maybe, one friend for a little while, once in a while. Baby, are you still my friend? Friendship dies in the night when no-one is looking and no-one can say later exactly what went wrong.

Why are people always staring? In the bus, on the streets, everywhere. They point their eyes at one and STARE! Walking with her she said *I've learnt to ignore them*. Well, I haven't.

I remember, many years ago, when I was a teen-ager, someone said to me: *you've got to learn to either soften the look in your eyes or desist from looking too strongly into girl's eyes. You confuse them. You make them think you're in love with them. You invite them to fall in love with you. You seem to promise them eternal, warm, caring love with your eyes.*

I smiled, slightly confused. But I knew she must know what she was saying. She was my cousin and knew my eyes and what lies ever behind them.

We went to the library, to check up on the progress and make final arrangements. I got there first. Every-thing, like almost always in Nigeria, is being rushed through in the last moments. The reading is on Satur-day. Yesterday was Monday, full of freshly awakened poetry. Everybody full of new lines, composed in their hearts over the weekend, strutting upon the stage, playing their parts, artistically, as though it wasn't all an act. Yesterday was Monday.

Monday, some say, is a slow day. Others say it is a fast day, hectic, with everything happening too fast for them to follow. It is, for some, a hard day, for others a dreamy one. Monday is an okay day, I guess. Afterall Monday is Sunday's child. Beautiful, deep Sunday. Land of answers.

She looked charged full of energy, as always. We collected the requisite material, first from the library, then from the publisher, then picked up a part of the decoration and headed for the venue. We spoke of this and that along the way, but said more with silence and thought thoughts than with words, spoken words. We really are close, a closeness many people would not understand. They would think of other things, as usual. And miss the very point.

We separate along the way, and meet again at the sponsors' and then return to the venue for the press conference.

Flow up and be free and be happy forever.

The Tool

...

THE LUST HUNG low in the air and looked for a tool. A passing slave, a temporary partner, an unwitting instrument with which to reach its constant goal; a bridge into the underground stream of earth-bound pleasure. A canvas on which to wreak and watch its own satisfaction satisfying itself.

How it woos you, how it stirs you, how it hovers around you and waits for an opportunity. It knows you well, knows that you will fall. You always fall. How many times have you been its bridge? The years have not altered you, they have only moulded you more thoroughly into the quiet tool of the lust.

For, see, again, the thought has occurred to you. You have indulged in the speculation. It is the bridge for which the lust has been waiting, waiting impatiently, nor did it have to wait for long.

Red, the embers, like the eyes of the lust. Faster than the speed of thought it opened the door and stood by the deeply hidden heavily breathing fireplace. See, how it blows the coal. See, how it fans the flames. Now they flicker, now they roar.

You lie down, a carnal bridge between two worlds, you spread yourself across the chasm, you arch yourself over the gulf. Those feet that step upon you, those palms that crawl, that stroking and slithering, it is the lust, as it passes over you, observing you amusedly, thirsting only after the pool on the other side. How sweet it is to be devoured by it as it passes you by...

How quickly it crossed over.

You turn around to look for it. One last look of amused contempt it threw your way, and then it quickly hurries on, leaving you cold, naked, shivering, used and spent, the lying bridge, beneath you only emptiness.

And as you ponder it again, empty and helpless, maybe exhilarated, maybe even ashamed, you hear its fleeing wings, feel its laughter; as you try to find your feet again, it has already deserted you, unquenchable vampire, and gone ahead to another, found another victim, another willing and unwitting tool. The sweet dark cloud. The lust. Hung on the ropes of consistent inconsistency, consciously dancing to the lust.

31. THE TOOL

Some say we're only human, and that our weakness is our innermost part. Some say the human's fallen and can't tell right from wrong. Some say the human being is only being human, and is simply growing, and it's all just a part of it. The sun sets and the sun rises, the lust hypnotises you once more with its chameleonic stare. You stare at one another quietly, and inside you you ask yourself: to which school of thought do I belong?

The Fluttering

...

OUTSIDE MY WINDOW there fluttered a bird...

I opened the window and in it flew. It alighted upon my table and became a story, a book of many pages full of emotion and history. Poet, poet, you anchored the story and it became a masterpiece that fed and accompanied human hearts from generation to generation.

There is an old book that began at the dawn of history and has no end, for from generation to generation there is always a poet to receive its next pages, humanity's rebirth, return of inspiration and guidance. The mystery, it seems to me, comes always in the shape of a bird and survives in the shape of a flower in the desert.

The bird kept on singing, narrating; I kept on listening, the poet kept on writing, the poet in me. When the last page emerged and the bird disappeared, a day of sharing passed, and I fell asleep.

A century of slumber passed again. Again again the night dawned and swallowed up the world. From the depths of my sleep a sound extracted me, the flutterings of a bird. Outside the window, woman or bird? Woman and bird? A woman stands behind the bird. With sleepy eyes I her behold, a waif of moonlight, standing outside my window, an ephemeral beauty, a strange maid...

I desire her. My desire becomes the magic wand with which she hypnotises me. I lose interest in the bird, the bringer of my stories, the being of my inspiration. Instead, I open the window and walk to the woman. Dimly I was aware of the bird that flew in through the open window of my soul into my chamber of secrets even as I walked out of it, into the hungry night. The glass door shut behind me, Noah's ark sailed away sans poet. There she stood before me, the night's promise, unfulfillable. A thousand pleasures she would give to me, but none quenched my thirst... Until it dawned that she was the thirst itself, cyclically renewing itself, fawn Sisyphus.

Wearily I dragged myself back to my window; shut. It was shut, long shut, with me on the outside. Looking in I make out, upon the table, another book, another distant story, buried in my heart. Like a visitor at a glass tomb, thoughtfully I look back in time.

It used to be a bird, a bird that once flew to me. Sadly I gaze at the scroll through the infinity of a glass window. I can see the book deep within my soul, but I cannot reach or read it. I stretch forth my yearnind hand, but all I manage to do is scratch the window pane with with my fingernails. Poet, poet, awakened and then distracted, unable to anchor your story, the very reason for your awakening. How does it feel to gaze upon your calling and be unable to enter it?

Weary and more you search until you find the door, and re-enter your inner home, but generations have since passed... the table, it is empty.

So here you go, sleeping again. A century and many more of restless dreams. Then, one day, you hear it... a familiar sound... outside your window... the Fluttering...

The night is dark, the moon is pale and sceptical, the glass is scratched, the witch is calling and the bird is fluttering...

Do you remember? It has been a long sleep. Memory has become a distant memory. Who is this moon? What is this woman? Why is this night? When is this window? How is this bird?... Even yourself you do not know anymore. Long was this sleep.

Poet, poet, you move in my heart, like a bird fluttering outside my window. Time is my window. If I open it and let the bird fly in, I will see and remember that it is no ordinary bird, it is a memory being, a fountain-pen, a poem, a story which, anchored, will grow wings and fly into the hearts of those who are thirsty outside...

Poet, poet, you speak in my heart. Forget that woman and face your true love.

The Cave of Contradictions

...

IS THERE A permanent state of strength? Life: a continuous battle against weaknesses.

A constant wishing to explore to what extent one can yield to weakness – and to what extent one can avoid the exertion of maximum effort – without endangering the goal. Testing the border. Touchline wizardry. A constant toying with the desire to yield to the temptation to redefine and rediscover an indolent optimum on a level of less-effort-more-pleasure.

It is a constant Sinning and hoping to get away with it. The tendency to sink back into sleep in the consciousness of the fact that only through the opposite of sleep – Effort – can there be progress. Wanting both. Wanting sleep and indulgence, wishing for progress. And vice versa. Human interior: cave of contradictions.

Indulgence. In the exercise of self-will and the experiencing of vanity. In the tasting and enjoying of the pleasures of Lust and physical Eros and the drunkenness of power; curiosity and propensity. Indulgence. In the reduction of effort and the inhalation of lethargy. And hoping, inspite of all this, to still do just enough in order to be able to attain goals, the path to which stands in the starkest contrast to such pernicious indulgence.

Should we expect people, including ourselves, to nobly and gallantly 'learn from their mistakes', and be surprised when at unexpected decisive crossroads the majority suddenly yield again and again to the same impulses which occasioned failure in the past?

Or should we expect it? Anticipating this behavioural pattern even as we work against it within ourselves, and allow ourselves to be surprised by the occasional absence of it, in the assumption man has not given up on his craving for primeval indulgence which he carries like a secret fragile treasure guarded inchoately deep within his being? The slumber shredded by the crack of dawn. The sleeping one arose not, rolling around in bed. Then came the soft dark clouds. Eden interruptus.

The smell of pleasure. Inhale. In the cave of contradictions.

Being Different

...

UNRAVELLING THE mystery that is my own soul, I pondered and sought; I wondered about my beginning. Woman and man in a garden. Which garden? East or west? Home is best, they say.

So I went home into my spirit-man and discovered an a different person dwelling within, staring back at me with my own face but not my own eyes.

"Different person," I asked him, "Who are you and what are you doing inside my heart?"

But he only returned my gaze without giving an answer, and I sensed that I must find the answer myself. Myself? But who is myself?

The mystery took shape, deepened, arose. I wandered from pole to pole. But each time I thought I had found my goal, I saw the different person inside my heart again, looking back at me with my own face but not with my own eyes.

I wanted to scream, but my heart rejected this. I lay me down to sleep, but sleep ejected me. So on and on I wander and sojourn, on and on I go, seeking to unravel this mystery that is simply my very own self.

And each time I think I have found the answer, I see him again, a different person inside my soul, staring back at me with my face but not with my eyes.

Who are you, I wonder, you stranger in my soul?

What are you, why are you, so different, so alien, so silent, so bold?

I Sing Another Song

...

I SING another song now. I hum another melody. I wander through distant fields and yet I never leave this body. I climb high mountains, cross stark deserts, span deep valleys, sail blue seas, search old forests, wander in thought, saunter through time and space.

I ask old questions, see new mysteries, hear low voices, whispering, whispering, catch strange smells, some low, some high, ponder secret numbers in my soul.

I dance to music which I alone hear, answer to calls which sound to none but me, bear ancient names which only I remember, call anew to spirits long and far gone, hoping they will tell me simply, in a language my heart remembers, the silent answers to the silent questions that flicker in my soul, and I never believe the lie.

And wonder I wonder, everyday I wonder: How can I tell you this without you thinking I am mad? Tell you that the bird you see, I do not see... the songs you sing, I do not hear... the times you remember, I never knew... without making you feel that I fear you might be mad?

My brother, we are different and yet but the same: two lonely souls talking, but the wind alone understands our speech, not us ourselves. We merely pretend that we understand us so that we both do not lose the only friend we have...

But, Friend, in the end you are simply you and I but I. So never think that I won't understand that I don't you. If there be one common Understanding which we share, it is but this: Every wanderer wanders alone.

A Private Affair

...

WE DECIDED TO let her have her affair, and pretended not to know.

We all work in the same office, she sits in front of her computer right at the back of the office, and computes away. We all sit in front of our computers, computing away.

I saw one of the first emails. It was one of those accidents that happen in the workplace. I don't know where she went to, I don't know what compelled me to get up and go to her empty desk, and click on. I shouldn't have. Seeing that she was not there, I should have just walked away; shouldn't even have gone there in the first place. But I was in a hurry, she should have forwarded the email to me an hour ago,

I needed information in it to help me finish the contract I was drafting for an agent, and the deadline was noon. Without thinking, I grabbed the mouse and began to browse her inbox which surprisingly was open on the screen. Normally she *always* locked her screen before she left her seat.

Suddenly I hesitated. She was a person who guarded her privacy intensely. She was a bit different from the rest of us in the office, at least in this regard. With any other colleague it would not have mattered, but she was... *Hmm*... Come to think of it, *what* did she have to hide anyway? Why was she *always* locking her screen? *Mchw!*

My annoyance at knowing I would have to let go of her PC without getting what I wanted, thereby facing the risk of not meeting my deadline, almost rubbed me of my morals. But still I hesitated, which in itself irritated me all the more. She was the only one in the office who guarded her privacy with such tenacity. But the moment of hesitation had done its job. I sighed. *Don't be a jerk!* I told myself, *she's different from the rest of us, just let her be*. I shook my head and started to turn away...

Then I saw the name. The email at the bottom of the page. It rang a shrill bell. I did a double-take. That name! But, even more than the name, was the subject title of the email. *"Babycakes, can't wait"*. Almost mechanically, without any conscious effort, I pointed the mouse at the incomprehension and clicked. The clarification came. I closed the email, returned the inbox to the face of the monitor and walked away, thoughtful, to my seat. She was having an affair. With *him.* It hit me like a thunderbolt.

For the better part of the next hour, my mind was in turmoil. Needless to say, I missed my deadline. Even when she returned to her seat five minutes after I left it, and eventually forwarded the email to me, I couldn't work. It took me a long while to find my composure.

For some reason I kept it to myself. Over the next couple of weeks, I began to observe her more closely. Such a quiet, shy, unassuming, unobtrusive personality. *Babycakes, can't wait.* How had it started? Every once in a while I would turn around, steal a glance at her, or watch her as she walked by. And each time, the wedding ring on her finger would catch my eye, and I would think of her four year old son who she once brought with her to the office. *Babycakes, can't wait.* What was she doing? I noticed that she began to receive lots of phone calls. Private phone calls on her mobile phone. Each time, she would jump up and hurry out of the office; and in between the phone calls, frequently, the buzz of incoming text messages. *Babycakes, can't wait.*

I don't know how the others came to know, truly I don't. Maybe because of all the sudden personal phone calls. One day, while she was out, we were all talking, and the conversation gravitated to love and affairs... and it turned out that we all knew she was having an affair... and with whom.

Maybe because none of us had ever met her husband. Maybe because all of us liked her, liked her quaint, quiet, modest personality. But we never discussed it again amongst ourselves. For some reason hard to explain, we all hushed it up.

The months passed. No one came to visit her in the office. Was she still having the affair? She remained her usual self, quiet, generous with friendly smiles. The phone calls and the text messages kept on coming, an insistent flood of private vibrations.

One day, her husband came to the office. I think that was when the pain of conflict drove all of us into intense inner reflection. He was a *nice* guy, with an unassuming, almost self-deprecating air, greeted everybody with a wide smile, an eager handshake. In the following days, we started to talk about her affair again. *It was moral, it was immoral, life is a mystery, she needs salvation, maybe he's doing it too, who knows how it really is in their home, it is a sin, everybody has free will, monogamy is unnatural, polygamy is unnatural, judge not, love thy neighbour, trust nobody, watch out for the devil, what a man can do a woman can do better, are we sure, maybe we're mistaken, stop gossiping, stop spreading rumours, it is true, I have the proof, the world is coming to an end, he must be doing her well, maybe her husband has stopped performing, it's his money she's after, but she's such a good girl, we must put her in our prayers, there must be a reason, love is a mystery...* As always we only spoke about it when she was not there. Was she still having the affair? I didn't know. I didn't ask.

And then came the day when everything changed. Her phone burped. A short conversation. A loud gasp. An ominous pause... and then it broke out: a frightening, low, howl that gripped every heart in the office. It seemed as though we all started up at once. I turned around. Her face was in her hands, she was sobbing. Wracking, ugly sounds, primitive and real.

I jumped up and hurried with the others towards her. It took a long time to calm her down. After she had shut down her computer and left, I walked into the toilet, to avoid the chatter of the colleagues. I put the seat down, sat on it, closed my eyes and watched again in my head the scene that had played out after we all rushed to her.

"What's wrong?" someone asked.

She sat frozen, staring at her mobile phone, as if hoping it would ring again. Her voice was a whisper:

"A friend of mine... just died... he took part in the fuel protest in Lagos today... he got hit by a stray bullet... his best friend was with him... "

Silence.

"What's his name?" someone whispered gently.

A pause.

"Kulie Oto."

"The artist?"

"The activist?"

"The lecturer?"

All three questions came at once.

She answered mechanically.

"Yes..., the sculptor. He is... was... my husband's cousin."

"Really?" Even I felt my eyebrow rise. She was still mumbling softly, almost to herself.

"He's the one who just called... I mean my husband... to tell me... there was some shooting... people ran... Chiya... was hit... fell... his best friend found him... I don't understand... he flew to Lagos yesterday evening... he was to travel back to Abuja this evening..." Her eyes travelled from mobile phone to PC screen and back again.

Babycakes, can't wait.

A very uncomfortable silence followed.

She breathed out slowly, very slowly. As if she was letting something out. She shook her head.

Silence. Longer.

And then:

"I'm so sorry for his wife and three children," someone said, evenly.

Months have passed again. The calls don't come

anymore. Her smiles are few and far-between. Somewhere in the quiet depth of her heart, her secret, her loss and her pain continue to rest, unshared. In the office nobody talks about it anymore. Silence has encapsuled it once more, like a matter that has been put to rest.

Yesterday's Faces

...

YESTERDAY, IT WAS as beautiful as the early morning sunlight dancing upon a rose. My heart was not my heart, but myself; and my face was not my face, but the shimmering reflection of my heart.

As I was striding once, I saw a figure hovering in the Air. But she had no wings, only the longest, most gleaming braids I ever saw, but gleaming not as bright as her eyes, eyes a-smiling straight into mine.

"Come, my friend," called she to me in voice of purest gold, "Follow me awhile and I will show you distant places of light and harmony, yes indeed I will!"

I nodded and right there and then her words lifted me up into the magic-coloured sky where, I by her side, we flew over two crystal mountains and one silver lake and then hovered a while above a garden where children wiser than the wisest men were building beautiful castles not in the air or sand, but inside their own hearts.

And then we flew off once again and this time when we paused, a circle of beautiful winged horses with talking eyes came flying up to meet us. We mounted two and journeyed on... but where we went from there I know not anymore, for I have lost my memories of then...

Because now I wonder, like one blind, in the dark and earthly worlds of modern men. And ever, when the sun is a-dawning, or a-shinning but not burning, though it be noon, or a-setting down, I ever and again go on long, gentle strolls, as though I were trying to recapture that glorious journey which I barely remember...

And today as I wandered through dingy markets I saw a *face*... a woman selling decaying fish, eyes materialistic and cunning, impure seduction. Of course she was not that beautiful Maiden of my all but forgotten past.

So why then does she look so familiar? And what was it that startled her when our eyes touched? Unsettled her. But of course she *cannot* be that same beautiful female spirit of ancient days who I left up in glorious heights yesterday...

I hope.

Bread

...

AND AS he was about to throw his daily alms at the beggar, he suddenly saw, not a coin, but a piece of bread in his palm... and this is what the inner voice said:

If you gave a person a piece of bread, just imagine for once if you were the one receiving this piece of bread. How would the entire event look to you? What would be going on in you? This will help you to have the right attitude, even as a giver. Especially as a giver. For sensitive and understanding must be the giver. Because it is a great burden to receive. So hand over this burden gently. Do not mock them that must receive from you, but remember too to preserve their dignity.

There is a common humanity that we share, and it is this shared oneness that interacts with itself each time we give and receive. And so, many times it is the giver who has actually received even more, often without even being aware of it. Give therefore with gratitude at the opportunity to give, you who receive all the time.

With what may you give? First of all, with understanding. Empathy. The urge and the attempt to truly understand the outer position and inner disposition of another awakens within one something which can be passed on to another.

Sometimes just a smile of encouragement, a look of warning, a question or a suggestion. A small gift. A favour, small to you but big to the recipient. Big to you but bigger still to the recipient. The culture of compassion. Edifier of the human race.

The art of giving and receiving. So fine an art. Giving without giving away our humanity. Receiving without receiving also indignity. Receiving without paying for it with even the subtlest of humiliation. Receiving objectively, careful not to take one-sidedly. Giving objectively, careful not to be one-sided. Giving without expecting in return anything else, anything lower, than the experiencing of a shared humanity. The giver knows gratitude too, a strange happy release of elated normalcy within one's heart. The perception that one has just done that for which one lives. To give.

And who can give the most? None other than the receiver. Oh, how much, how so much the receiver could give, more than he knows. He can give to the occasion the height of dignity it deserves by receiving with dignity, maturity and freedom. To receive does not mean to be a slave for life – but to receive is to create a kind of temporary internal imbalance which urges towards restitution. And this alone is released in Gratitude. When you receive you must give something back. This is also the law of reciprocal action. You must give back, according to your nature.

Behold this beautiful Creation that issued forth from the Spirit of God. Forever it returns to us the fruits of our thoughts and words, the results of our deeds and even our most intuitive perceptions. We reap what we sow. Pleasure and pain. Joy and sorrow. Growth and limitation. Everything comes back in the Law of Reciprocal Action. Forever we receive. Receive back.

And forever we must give. Give back in the service of Growth. Like the recurrent seasons, so does the urge make itself felt over and over again within us deeply. The urge to give, to give of ourselves. The urge to give to others the honest effort to understand them; to really try to understand others. This is the foundation of all proper Giving. This is the beginning of giving. Understanding is the first step towards Giving. And it lies in our nature.

It does not lie in our nature to return hatred for hatred, darkness for darkness. These are alien to that which makes us fruits of an ever onward evolving Creation of Light. But it lies in our nature, more or less deeply buried, to look into the heart of things and sense what we owe each thing – gentleness or severity, a question or an answer, a gift or a demand, a favour or a waiting upon a something that ought to have come. Or laughter or quiet. Or just plain Gratitude. It lies in our nature to seek for understanding, and then to act, to give, from out of this Understanding. This is the meaning of life.

In that piece of bread you are about to give lies an opportunity to give that which makes us all human. It is the bread of life. Have your bite and pass it on. It will come back to you, richer and fuller. But keep it for yourself, and it will disappear like a thief into the night. You will seek It, but It will remain as elusive as the Holy Grail. But find love within you, and seek to give love to those around you, and It will come to you.

He looked down at his palm again, and saw his daily alms, waiting to be thrown.

The Madman

...

SOMETIMES I wonder, by the look in their eyes, if indeed I am crazy. The conclusion almost becomes a certainty – crazy I must be. Or wherefore the baffling communication gaps, the startling differences of opinion, all the way down to the ground level? Indeed I must be the insane and they the sane. "The majority is not always right!" is the cry of every outlaw and every lunatic, the defence of every man who cannot swing with the times.

Thus I am almost certain... lunacy is my bane, my fate, my reality which I scarce will accept! When they turn left, I turn right. When they go up, I descend. When I express my heart, it renders theirs a-broken and when I dance in joy, they dance upon the china of my desires and leave me equally a-shattered.

When I fain will spread my wings, spread my wings and fly, they get alarmed lest I fall and break my neck, and so they move to stop me, even if it means they must clip me my wings...

And yesterday I saw them moving towards the precipice and I screamed and warned, then watched, heart in mouth, but – *what do you know?* – when the smoke had cleared I saw them standing, smiling, on the *other* side of the gorge.

Mysteries.

So I decided to follow them too, follow them over yon yawning cleft... I took a step and, strange to say, the white smoke did not encircle me too, nor did I float, but I pummelled headlong down the limitless chasms, rushing towards my death. – O Father, save me, was my Prayer! – and my wings, the wings I had *let* them clip, they sprouted afresh and I flew me out into the world whence I had departed; and then into other realms calling me from new distances.

And even until today I am yet to be ever enclosed by those clouds that lifted them across their gorge...

A Mountain's Peaks

...

LET ME tell another short story. I know the bird is on its way. The cloud told me so. The cloud heard it from another cloud, who heard it from another cloud, who heard it from another cloud, from cloud to cloud to cloud the message was whispered until it made its way to me, the mountain-peak: the bird is coming.

Yes, I am rock, here up above I live. I am the mountain-peak. I have existed longer then you can imagine, you this earthman writing down my words for me now. Today you write my story. Tomorrow you will be gone and I will call another poet to me who will be my new biographer, and through him or her my story shall continue to flow...

You deem me static, solitary. I am neither. I have

been where you have never been, places in space, points in time. Aye, I have been where you have never been, for I was not born today. I know you better than you know yourself, dear poet, far far better.

Nor am I solitary. I have friends whose nature you cannot conceive of. I speak with them that lie beyond the limit of you and your earthly perceptions. They visit me everyday and we go on long walks through dimensions that are mine alone to explore.

I am the mountain-peak. *I* told you the story of the killer-horses and the flying ponies. *I* told you the story of the blind stream. *I* told you the story unwritten. I have seen the old book unfolding since the dawn of man, for I am a part of it. Now I want to tell you one more thing, dear poet; - if you touch my heart and touch it so deeply that I melt and flow, I will put a part of my mountain in you. And when you come back to the earth, if you ever choose to, if you ever have to, you will be my pen again and we shall write newer stories and unveil older beginnings and the ancient shall be the finishing point where we close our cycle, open our future. We shall be another arising...

Now go, dear poet, and leave me in peace. The gentle clouds that massage and caress my crown have brought me good news this day. I shake. I quake. I can barely bear the joy that consumes me, seeking to burst forth. I shudder. Ah, what is this? Tears. I shed tears... Again, I do. – until my heart is calm, my ears

clear; mountain-peak, I stand and await with a smile
and a song the arrival of the bird.

Trees Alone, Stand

...

THE STORY of two *udara* trees. Arose together, lived together, aged together. Their roots were entangled beneath the surface of the earth, where no eyes could reach, wonder and question.

Do you know how it is when you try your utmost best to accomplish a feat and then, just before you acieve your aim, failure appears from around the corner, gives you a knowing smile, and you know you lost?

Now this is actually a game that failure likes to play. You have not actually lost – yet. Not yet. But if you hesitate too long, you're gone.

They loved each oher to the end of time, the two

udara trees, but time has no end. Or if it has, no-one has got there yet and come back to tell.

Does it surprise you how hard it is for you to tear yourself away from me? You are paying too much attention to the knowing smile on failure's face. But our roots are locked firmly together, beneath the soil, where no eyes can see, not even failure's deceptive peer. Let that be a comfort to you.

But if we say sometimes yes, sometimes no, sometimes... yes sometimes no sometimes yes...

Paper Men

...

PAPER MEN adorn the earth. When they fall in water, they weaken and are soon in threaded bits. When they meet with fire, they are speedily scorched and have no resistance to offer. When heavy hands grab them, they are easily torn and shorn, and the wind effortlessly blows them around, in bits or whole. And rub them hard upon the earth the way you'd rub a stone, you'd watch them pale and wither and assume ugly contours.

Unlike trees they cannot weather the wind... unlike swords they conquer not fire... unlike sand they cannot tease rough waters... and unlike diamonds they never rest easy in the earth.

And yet, when Angels will put down their lofty

thoughts into the world of humans, they do so but upon the souls of those who are plain and open, like paper, and the world revers her poets forevermore.

Goodbye - Welcome

...

ONCE UPON A time three ants ran across a wall. They all got crushed by the same hand and died. The hand put itself into food and fed the mouth, and the owner of hand and mouth died because the ants were rare and poisonous. Those who buried the corpse fell ill and died too because the poison was spreading. Nobody buried them. Birds of prey fed on them and later fell down dead from the sky. Goats and cows fed on the grass near the dead birds and, before they died, men drank of their milk; the goats and cows died and the disease was back in the lives of men.

People were dying left and right everyday. From where had this unknown disease come? Where was it headed? Would it move on and leave us alone or would it stay or would it take us along?

But there was a breed of people who did not die, against whom the poison held no sting, in whose land the power of the disease was broken. And all those who knew, or found, and walked the way into their land, this inner state of being, overcame the death that lives through our folly.

Goodbye.

Welcome.

In Our Desert

...

BIGOTRY CONTINUES to exist upon the face of the earth, but not within its heart. And just as skin-characteristics are skin-deep, so is bigotry only surface-deep. I'm talking about the face of the earth.

But anyone who nurtures bigotry within the heart will continue to nourish it for a long time yet to come. It will not die easily. Is there hope for the flower?

Should I revert to the tales of the heart? Should I revert to the inner sequence? Should I revert to yesterday's tenderness? The first woman? The last kiss?

Or should I continue into the desert? Should I seek a new oasis and wander after the unknown treasures of the sand? But who can open up the secrets of the sand? A flower?

The first strike was a miss. The first step was the first fall. The first sight was blinded by a pitch-fork. But there will be a second. The second is the other side of the coin.

I want to write a poem. I want to penetrate deep into the heart of the broken home, there where the spirit in us resides. We are all to one another strangers. Bridges we build, communal words we use, eyes we touch when we will, hands we give, yet remain unto one another strangers. The shared blood was poisoned aye ere we were born. The shared earth was divided already long ago and divided we stand and stare at one another across the border, the boundaries of our little egos and remain each alone. But each is but alone. Little egos. Little worlds. Little by little, if watered, like flowers, perhaps, we grow.

The secrets of the sand, approaching, covering up our footsteps. Hey, I wrote this poem before, when I was young. But if I was young then, what am I now, older or younger? For the first poem was the greater and the latter flow gropes for reconnection with the source that thundered out of the young heart of the finalised decision. Seen once. Pondered once. Grasped once. Perceived once. Decided once. At the start of the journey. And everything else is just the hanging on, the wondering, the new search. We have found but have not yet reached the Goal. We are still on the path. Believing in the flower.

This is what I would like to give to you, a flower in the desert. Do not perhaps think that the Desert is more powerful than the flower. Nay. There you would err. But treasure and protect the flower. Water it anywhere you see it. For the flower alone, of all the forces in the universe, can subdue the Desert.

Fruits

...

IN MY village, beneath the *ụdara* trees when the sun is setting, a man from the city sits with a book in his hands, under a certain tree. His book is empty, but each time he opens it it quickly and magically fills with words; and then he sells it to the world.

So, with empty books, we sat down on his favourite spot. But our books stayed empty. The man said:

"The author is the book, the book just the reader."

"And this tree?" we asked him.

He looked up in surprise:

"Oh, I never noticed the tree before."

"It is visible only when you are sitting under it!"

And he gazed at the tree and became thoughtful.

There is
always
something
more